BILLIONAIRE ON AIR

BILLIONAIRE MATCHMAKER
BOOK FIVE

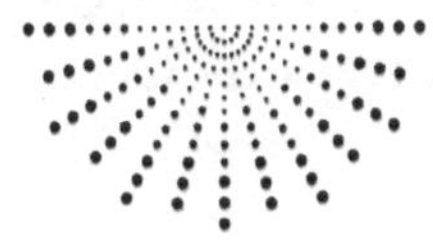

SUMMER COOPER

LOVY BOOKS

CHAPTER ONE

LANEY

"What do you mean you're too old? Girl, you're only twenty-four, you're still a baby! Wait until you're my age, then you'll know what old is!"

The harsh words were softened by a cackle of laughter and twinkling blue eyes, just a shade lighter than mine. Her eyes were rheumy with time and the strain of macular degeneration, but still beautiful.

"I should shoo you off my front porch, Mrs. Mallory. My day wasn't that bad really." I paused to rub the ache in my back. "I only fell down the steepest steps on campus and made a fool of myself."

"That doesn't mean you're too old for a blind date, dear girl. Now, my grandson will be back from that nerd convention next week and he's moving down to the basement apartment." I saw she'd let that slip without thinking and tried not to grin as she tried to backtrack.

"I mean from his business meeting. You just let me know if you change your mind, alright? He needs to make some friends so he won't turn into a hermit down there."

I hated blind dates and knew she probably just wanted to dump her freeloader—I mean, *grandson*—on me but decided to be polite. "I certainly will, Mrs. Mallory. I haven't in the last few years, but you never know, right? Do you want to stay for dinner?"

Mrs. Mallory lived alone and often ate with my roommate and me, or we could be found at her house. We'd kind of all adopted each other, all of us without family in our little slice of Albertsville on the southern coast of South Carolina. She lived in a tiny house painted light blue with dark blue trim between the Victorian palace to her left and us in our not quite palace on the right. We did have a window seat, though, in one of those round bay windows that always have window seats. It must have been obligatory. I have to admit, it was my favorite room in the two-story house.

I waited for her answer as she sipped at her sweet tea, her eyes dancing with the delightful little secret she was about to tell me. For an elderly lady, Mrs. Mallory was active, fun-loving, and delighted in telling secrets, even her own.

"No, I'm heading out to the club for bingo night." The pale widow, a small, bent woman with silvery white hair in a loose bun on the back of her head, gave me a wink. "Mr. Sandford is sneaking in the gin tonight."

I gave a bark of laughter at the naughtiness of sneaking gin into an old folks' club to party while playing bingo and took her hand. "You know I love you, don't you?"

"Don't be sassy, girl!" She gave me a stern look with pursed lips but the corners of her lips tilted as she looked down at me from the porch swing. "Don't wait up for me tonight!"

I laughed again as she left the porch, her seventy-year-old legs quickly carrying her away. I might not be too old for a blind date, according to Jane Mallory, but I was too old for falling down stairs. I promised myself I'd take online classes next semester as I gathered up empty glasses of iced tea and went into the house I shared with my best friend.

"Tony? Have you seen my glasses? I could have sworn they were on my head, but they aren't," I called to my roommate and waited for an answer as I rinsed the glasses.

"Laney, you need some of those string-things little old church ladies use. You're constantly losing those things, I don't know why you don't just get contacts!" Tony came into the kitchen, his light hazel eyes amused as he brought me the green plastic-framed glasses I'd been looking for since I came home. "You left them on the bathroom sink again, sweetie."

I smiled at him gratefully and kissed his coffee-colored cheek. "You're my hero!"

He tilted his head imperiously before he went to the fridge and pulled out a juice box. We liked apple juice more than pop and buying it in juice boxes just seemed sensible. Plus, I'll admit, we kind of liked the childishness of it, the memory of being a kid returned every time we opened one.

"I have a date tonight with Justin. What are you going to do?" He took a delicate sip from the straw, his handsome face a picture as he grinned at me.

"Justin, huh? I won't expect you home until morning then!" I studiously ignored his question and took out a microwave meal.

I hated them but on the nights when Tony went out on dates it was only me. I popped it into the microwave and waited. I knew he'd ask again.

"No dates tonight, Laney?" His deep voice was so soothing most of the time that I always told him he should be a radio DJ, but when he got into one of his 'you need to date' moods, I just wanted to strangle him.

"Why can't I just date you, Tony?" I asked, knowing it was impossible.

"Well, if you want to spend that kind of money and become a man, honey, you're welcome to it, but I got plenty of those. And you got plenty of what you need to find the right man to do the job for you, if you'd only let somebody do it." He gave me a pointed look as he finished his juice box and tossed it in the trash.

"I'll worry about it when I finish this law degree. Right now, I don't want to be distracted by a man, or do something stupid like get pregnant. I just don't feel that... *need* to have a man." It was a lie, but he didn't need to know that.

I'd been alone for so long, I'd learned to deal with my needs, even if I sometimes felt like crawling into the nearest bar and picking up a stranger just to feel someone touching me. I really didn't want the distraction, though, so most nights I did what I could to relieve the ache by myself. There was no shame in it, and it kept me on the straight and narrow. Plus, I did a much better job alone than any past lover had. Tony didn't need to know that, though.

"Well, you know what I think about that." He gave me another pointed look. "You can't be alone forever you know. You'll dry up and blow away and youth is only for the young. You'd better use it while you can."

I gave him a grim look and turned to the microwave, my arms wrapped over my generous breasts. I'd been lucky in the body department; I had a curvy figure with a big ass, a slim waist, and large breasts. I sometimes thought I looked like the women in those Rubenesque paintings, but then I'd tell myself I need to find exercises to pare down my big ass, as running every day just wasn't doing it. Then, I walk away from the mirror and go back to my books and all my self-doubts and recriminations disappear.

I was a scholar, an academic, and law was my area of expertise. I was confident in the classroom and in every aspect of the law, but out in the real world—in the world of dating and sex—I mostly kept to myself.

"I'll find a man when the time is right, Tony Mason, not a moment before." I took the cardboard box of molten chicken alfredo with broccoli out of the microwave and set it on the table. "Now, let me enjoy my frozen-centered dinner and go away."

I gave a wave of my hand and Tony laughed. "I love you, girl. Don't ever change."

"I love you too, now go do nasty things with dirty people. Just make sure you tell me all the gory details later!" I did love to hear his stories of seduction and lust, even if I didn't have my own to share back.

"You know I will," he called as he headed out of the door to drive away.

I'd met Tony a few years before at a local flea market as we bargained with a vendor over a rug. He kept offering more than I did, both of us laughing, and I finally caved, saying I didn't have anywhere to put the handmade woven grass rug anyway. He'd looked at me and asked if I was homeless, and I told him about how I'd been staying in a ratty hotel when my student housing burned down one night. The university was doing all they could to re-house the other four girls I'd shared with, but nothing was happening fast. He'd told me about his house on one of the old Charleston streets, an inheritance from his grandmother, and we'd been roommates since.

I ate my crappy meal in silence and planned out the paper I needed to start writing. I was almost finished with my law degree. Tony barely charged me rent and my job at the library as a helper three days a week kept me in pocket money. My parents were paying for my education but I'd insisted on doing the rest on my own. My mom still tried to slip money into my bank account without me knowing about it, going to our local bank in Greenville to make a deposit every now and then, but I never asked for it. She thought I was still unaware of where the money came from, but I knew.

They were proud of their only child, and Mom used her earnings as a cardiologist to make sure I had a bright future. I paid them back by studying hard. Except for the time I missed when I contracted meningitis during an outbreak at the university, I spent all of my time studying. Now that I could see the finish line, I didn't want to let up the pace.

Tony tempted me most days with tales of a new club

he'd found, and the men and women that went to it. I'd almost caved a few times, but I'd found the will to turn it down. This redhead wanted her law degree, not a man! I'd provide for myself, and I'd never have to depend on anyone but me.

With a sigh, I went to my books, opened my laptop, and got back to work. An hour later I was making brownies, promising myself I'd run an extra two miles in the morning. It was going to be one of those long nights where I wished like hell I'd gone out with Tony, but some fudgy brownies would do the trick instead. Or so I told myself.

I flipped through the television channels as I waited, rolling my eyes at the garbage that passed for television now. I'd grown up watching stuff many would consider ancient, black and white television shows about witches and genies, stuff that had a plot, and some more modern shows but I hated reality television of any kind. Except for documentaries, and even those were driving me up the wall lately. Conjecture stated as fact, opinions given as proof, it just made me doubt the whole program so I usually just stopped watching.

I saw one of those dating programs, the kind where women vie for the attention of some billionaire, and had to fight the urge to pull a face. Those were so fake! How anyone believed they were real was beyond me. It was all fake, right down to the marriage that came later, the pregnancy, and then the divorce once the limelight was off the nationally loved couple. You couldn't learn to love someone in just a matter of weeks, there was just no way.

I settled on a horror program about a town where the people went crazy one by one and the people try to avoid the madness, whilst waiting for my brownies to bake. I took a call from my mother, telling her about Mrs. Mallory's gin-soaked plans, and listened to her as she told me about the neighbor's cat using her new hot tub as a water bowl before it fell in. We talked about my classes and then she went off to make a cake for my father. We were a baking family, despite Mom being a cardiologist. We weren't very good at taking doctor's orders, obviously.

I went back to my paper and forgot about men, dating, and drunken passion. I had plans and they were focused on my law degree. I had to stay focused on that.

"LANEY, have you seen Mrs. Mallory's grandson from the front? If it lives up to the promise of the back I might just have to walk on over there and find out if he wants to see what my bedroom ceiling looks like." Tony was standing at the sink, washing dishes in a rather distracted manner.

I walked up behind him to look out of the window but all I caught was a glimpse of the newly arrived grandson as he went down to his basement apartment. He'd moved in a few days ago but I still hadn't met him. Mrs. Mallory was more than willing to set us up, but I'd been putting her off from the start. I knew she meant well, but the man was moving into his granny's basement. He was probably already in debt up to his eyeballs or such a loner that we'd share an awkward date over a pizza while he told me about his video game character all night.

Ugh, no, I couldn't deal with that kind of mess. Even if he did look good from the back.

"I haven't seen him from the front, I've been too busy with that paper. Maybe you should ask his gran to set you up," I said, hiding a grin behind my hand with a fake yawn. I turned away, the dazzle of the morning light hurting my eyes. He hadn't looked too bad from the back, but I squashed that thought.

"Oh no, sweetie, that's all about you. Tony don't do blind dates. Not with this body." He ran hands covered in brightly colored yellow gloves down his sides and flicked his head like he was tossing back long hair.

"You are a fine-looking man, baby. If only you weren't gay!" We laughed, the inside joke being how so many women told him that.

"Have I ever told you I'm glad you're just a nerd. A

damn sexy one." He paused to look me over in my yoga pants and oversized sweatshirt. "Even in that getup, but still a nerd. Which reminds me."

He wandered over to the shelf where we put the mail every day and used a finger to push through the pile to find his. I saw him grin widely before he snatched an envelope up and stuck it in the back pocket of his jeans. Tony gave me a wink as he went back to the dishes, his lips still smiling.

"Fun times ahead, so much fun."

I gave him a puzzled look but didn't ask. It was his business. Even if I did wonder what about my clothes reminded him he needed to check the mail.

"Well, I have to go to work so if you don't need me for lusting after the neighbor anymore..." I let the sentence trail off, waiting for his response.

"Girl, get to work. I need some new shoes this week." He gave me a wink to soften the words, and I gave him a slight hug and pecked his cheek before I went to change into more suitable attire.

"I'll see you this evening then."

I heard him chuckle as I left the room, and it made me wonder what he had up his sleeve. That gleam in his eye usually meant he had a plot afoot. Sometimes I was dragged into those plots kicking and screaming, but most of the time he'd go off and do whatever he was doing without me being any wiser. It kept our relationship fresh, what can I say? I never knew exactly what he was up to. He was my roommate and my best friend, not my boyfriend.

I went through my day finding research materials for students, logging books in and out, and even broke up a fight as two girls decided to fight over the same romance novel that it turned out we had several copies of, if they'd only asked. I drove home, my thoughts on a chilled glass of wine and a quiet story. I'd found this website where voice actors produced short stories, like the old-fashioned radio programs, and I listened to them almost every night now before bed. I found it soothing to listen as the readers got into the story and started really acting like the character as they spoke. It was good stuff to fall asleep to.

I knew Tony must be out before I even saw his car missing from the driveway, only the lamps were on throughout the house, the wall lights had all been left off. When I walked through the door I went through my normal routine, letting my hair down, kicking off my shoes and putting my purse down on the hall table, a masterpiece of reclaimed pine wood Tony had created from used pallets, and headed for the kitchen for that glass of wine.

There was already a wineglass on the kitchen island, with what looked a folded letter leaning against it. Curious, I picked it up. My heart started to race when I saw the letterhead... *Dream Matchmakers*. Tony wouldn't, would he? He would never...

Oh my God!

He had! Tony had managed to get me on a television dating show. He was so going to have to die!

CHAPTER TWO

JAKE

I shuffled through a list of things I had to do in the next couple of days and ignored the tone from my smart phone telling me I had another email. It was only a message from a dating website my gran had signed me up for. Women knew I had money after a little online research and were only interested in me for my bank account. Gran meant well, but all those women sending me naked pictures, offering to do *anything* for me, didn't turn me on. Besides, I knew they really wanted my wallet, not me.

"Jake, are you down there, my boy?" I heard Gran at the top of the stairs and walked up to see what she needed.

"What's up, Gran?" I pushed my dark brown hair out of my eyes and peered at her. The long length of my hair irritated her, and she sometimes walked around trying to cut it with a pair of scissors without me noticing. I'd been keeping it tied up in a protective bun since I'd moved back in with her, but hadn't bothered with it today. The tight buns always gave me a headache. Maybe it was time to cut it.

"It's so nice to be able to see those green eyes without all of that hair in the way. Why don't you let me cut a little off, Jake?" Gran turned away, waving her hand at me to follow.

"I might one day but not today. What may I help you with?" I grinned at her as she turned around and gave me a speculative look.

"You sassing me, boy?" She watched me and my grin deepened.

"Would I do that, Gran?" I blinked my eyes innocently.

"Of course, you would! Listen, I got some news in the mail today. Have a seat." She indicated a chair at the table next to the large window in the kitchen. The top of the walnut table was covered in papers, bottles of herbal supplements, and a small television she used to watch her game shows on. Gran wasn't one for technology, and now that she was older she didn't move around the house as much as she used to.

The table had always been her favorite place, even when I was a child. She'd taken me in after my parents died in a house fire, and I owed her the world. I'd moved back in with her recently, the need for privacy tantamount after I'd made my first billion dollars from my tech company and people started crawling out of the woodwork begging for money.

I'd been raised by a woman who loved the simple life. When she wouldn't move in with me to a gated house with a security guard, I thought the safest place to be was at her house. That was a great idea until she decided to sign me up to a dating website. How she'd even managed to get on the website, I had no idea, but she'd managed it. The woman didn't even own an analog cellphone! At least she hadn't listed my address or my alias. She'd used my real name, Jackson, and that's why they all thought I was still living in Charlotte, looking for a soul mate. In my business dealings, I used my full name, but in my everyday life, I went by Jake, which is what she tended to call me.

"Now, Jake, I know you may not like this, but, well..." Her words trailed off and she looked out of the window at the house next door for a moment. "Well, you need a woman, son! Or a man, but you need a partner! I guess there's no better way to say this than to just come out with it. I've signed you up for a television dating show. This is the paperwork."

I rocked back in my chair. The movement of my large, powerful frame made the chair creak ominously. I quickly moved back, leaning my elbows on the table. "You've done what now, Gran?"

"Here, look at this. And take your elbows off the table, it's rude!" She batted at my arms with her frail hands and I did as I was told. She'd never told me why it was considered rude to put your elbows on the table but she always said it was.

I pulled what looked like a thick report over to my side of the table and looked at it with dread. "What have you done now, Gran?"

"Oh, you're going to die a lonely old man at the rate you're going, down in that basement, Jake. I thought you could use a little excitement and I might have finagled you into a dating game show." She was looking at me from the side of her blue eyes, her lips twitching in absolute joy.

I took a deep breath and reminded myself that Gran loved me and that I loved her. She hadn't done this to hurt me, and though I really wanted to be angry I couldn't refuse her. She'd raised me, after all.

"It's that new one, where they have three men and one's rich, and nobody else knows but the three men and the show, which one is the rich one. You've hidden your status so people won't realize it's you, if you play your cards right. They think you're perfect for the show." She finally looked at me, her expression revealing her enjoyment at the thought of the game.

"You know this isn't my idea of fun, right, Gran?" I put the folder back on the table, wishing it would just go away.

So I'd made an absolute fortune with my tech company, that didn't mean I needed a wife, or even a woman for that matter, did it? I wanted to focus on the projects I had lined up, especially the one that would see teachers providing education to children in remote parts of the world through the use of solar-powered devices made from discarded tablets and phones. People threw away goldmines and didn't even know it.

"Gran, I just..." I paused as she looked at me with that look only a grandmother can give you, expectations of great things tinged with a slight disappointment that her world was about to cave in as reality dropped a bomb on her. "I don't know if I have time for this, Gran."

"Oh, boy, come on. You're down there in that basement all day long, fiddling with your toys, you have the time!" She smacked the tabletop for emphasis and I winced.

Those "toys" were my phone, tablet, and computer, from which I ran an empire without so much as ever stepping foot into an office. It wasn't that I was a recluse, I just hated wasting resources, resources that could be saved by not commuting and by holding meetings over the Internet or through video calls.

Forcing air out through my lips I looked at Gran. She

looked so hopeful, so pleased with herself, that I just couldn't say no. I didn't want to spend weeks being groped by a bevy of beautiful women that only wanted me because they thought I had a lot of money. Gran wanted it though so…

"Alright, fine, as long as I can keep working I'll do it." I didn't even realize I'd talked myself into the whole thing, Gran hadn't said a word.

"Great! You just need to contact this lady here at this email address and they'll get everything sorted. Oh, and read the contract." Gran patted the table this time, as if to apologize for the slap earlier, and went to put some coffee on. I had a feeling I'd need it.

* * *

"THIRTY SECONDS PEOPLE." A man with a pair of headphones on and a beard that would do Merlin proud walked past, holding up three fingers to the men gathered in the foyer of the rented mansion.

A few weeks after Gran had hoodwinked me into agreeing to this farce, I was stood under blazing lights in a tuxedo that was way too tight around my pectoral muscles, trying to hold a bland expression on my face. The papers had all been signed, I'd flown out to the island on a helicopter with the other men, and the three of us were now standing at the bottom of some schoolgirl's fantasy of a staircase, awaiting the entry of the female contestants.

The room went silent as Skip Norton, the congenial host of the show, came in through a doorway and started to speak. Wearing a white tux of his own with his black hair slicked back and blue eyes shining, the host walked around the room with cameras following, his 100-watt smile turned up to a million, almost blinding us.

"Tonight, we're coming to you live from Fountainhead Island, a tiny island off the coast of South Carolina and let me tell you, folks, it is truly paradise. Here at Fountainhead House we're about to meet our contestants, three handsome devils and twelve of the most beautiful ladies this great nation has to offer. Three of those ladies will find their Prince Charming here at Fountainhead Island and one lucky lady is going to win it all, a chance to marry a billionaire. Let's meet our eligible bachelors. Can you pick out which one it is?"

Skip walked to our side of the room and turned his smile up even more as he approached the third man in our small group.

"Tell us a little about yourself, sir, but not too much." Skip pointed a wink at the camera before he turned back to the man I knew to be Trent.

We'd all spent time together over the last few days,

working on our strategy for keeping our true pasts behind us. We weren't supposed to reveal anything about our jobs, that was all down to the show to reveal at the end, but we could talk about our pasts, family history, and things like that. I felt my palms go sweaty as Skip talked with Trent, and I kept glancing at the staircase waiting for the ladies to come down. Was my fair lady in the group of women I could hear giggling upstairs earlier in the day?

"I'm Trent, I'm twenty-six years old, and I couldn't be more pleased to be here tonight, Skip." Trent gave the camera a gleam of his own, and I knew the ladies would be falling all over him. He looked a bit like one of the British princes that were always being splashed across tabloid magazines.

It was hard not to roll my eyes as the man carried off his tux expertly and looked every bit the part of a billionaire, right down to the incredible smile he gave the cameras. Ladies were going to eat him in TV land.

"And what about you, sir?" Skip moved along, another wink at the ready.

"I'm David, twenty-five, and ready to get this party started, Skip! Bring on the ladies!" David gave a whoop and a fist pump, a move that could work both ways. The ladies and viewers would either be instantly turned off by such common behavior, or they'd accept it as the typical shenanigans of the very rich.

Skip gave David an odd look, one that said, 'take it down a notch', and moved along to me.

"You're awfully quiet down here, young man. Speak up or we'll forget you're down here." Another gleam at the cameras and Skip turned back to me.

I knew all of these men were performing for the camera and decided my best strategy was to just be myself. Skip would go back to the sour drunkard he was, David would put his nose right back into a book as soon the cameras went off, and Trent, well, I wasn't exactly sure why Trent was here. I was fairly certain he batted for the other team.

"Hi, Skip, I'm Jake and I can't wait to see what the night has in store for all of us as we meet our lovely ladies." I gave what I knew to be a genuine smile and kept my eyes off the cameras. We'd been warned not to look at them a thousand times since we'd arrived.

I still wasn't used to it all, but I'd give it a shot. Gran was counting on me to not only play along and help to build the mystery, but the show had me in chains about the whole thing too. Play by their rules or I'd be screwed over a barrel.

"There you have it, folks, three gorgeous men, one a plumber, one a teacher, and the other is, well, one of the richest men on the planet. Can you decide which that is yet? For now, let's meet our ladies, shall we?" Skip gave the cameras another gleaming smile, something I knew to be quite fake because the man seemed to hate life in general.

The music that had been tinkling through the room now increased in tempo, a sweeping orchestral sound, and the first lady appeared.

"Wow!" I heard David whisper beside me. I knew he'd be pushing his glasses up his nose right now if the producers hadn't forced him to wear contacts. His hand still came up, a sign of just how strong the habit was.

A lithe blonde came to the top of the grand staircase, a wide landing at the top. She paused there, her sapphire blue ball gown shimmering around her.

I glanced over at Trent and wasn't surprised to see just how bored he looked. Not his type then.

"Hi there, I'm Samantha, I'm twenty-two years old, a bartender, and I love to travel the world." Her smile could have rivaled Skip's for wattage but there just wasn't anything in it, another similarity to Skip.

Another woman, a redhead in an emerald ball gown took her place as the first lady descended the step.

"I'm Kelly, twenty-one, a physical therapy student, and I love to write poetry." Ah, an Irish lass then. A girl after my own heart. Her blue eyes gleamed as she started her own descent and I smiled up at her, liking her self-assured stare as she glanced over Trent, David, and me.

"Hey y'all, I'm Abby, twenty-six, and I love sky-diving." A brunette with a copper gown took Kelly's place and waved as she came down. A true southern belle.

I forgot the first three and the remaining eight as the woman of my dreams stepped onto the landing. Another redhead with light blue eyes, decked out in a golden ballgown. She took my breath away.

"Hi, uh, I'm Laney, I'm twenty-four, and I love, well, life in general. It's great, isn't it?" She gave a nervous smile, her eyes darting around until they met mine.

I saw her lips part in a silent "oh" and felt much the same way. She's the one, has to be. No doubt about it.

The ladies were all settling down on couches spread around the room, their nervous shifting creating a swishing sound as their gowns brushed against the couches.

I didn't know who any of the other girls were, or what they loved in life, because Laney had my full attention.

CHAPTER THREE

LANEY

I watched the other girls descend the stairs and clasped my hands in my lap. I sat still, the yellow silk of my dress quiet in a sea of rustling noises. I was nervous but calm. I'd somehow let Tony talk me into this farce. He'd even arranged with my boss at the library to allow me time off over the Thanksgiving break to film the show. We had two weeks to prove we were the one to whichever man we chose.

One of them was a very rich man, and we wouldn't know which it was until the last day, when the men made their choice. I felt like a zoo animal on parade and a fool for agreeing to the whole charade. I was here now, nothing I could do about it, so I sat and waited, my eyes darting between the man with the haunting eyes and the staircase.

I'd seen him first and hadn't been able to look away

as I came down the stairs. I almost tripped at the bottom, which had broken the spell, and I'd realized I'd stared at the gorgeous man far too long. He was tall, handsome, and his eyes. Dear God, his eyes were powerful. A light green rimmed with black lashes, they looked deep into my soul and I wanted to drown in them. His hair was short but it was still long enough to make my fingers twitch to touch it! It looked so silky.

I gave myself a mental shake as I realized I was ogling the man and looked down at my hands clenched together in white satin gloves. We'd all been given the same costume, though our dresses were in different jewel-tones, and our hair was all done in an upsweep, except for the girl with short hair. I think we were supposed to look like genteel and demure southern belles. I wanted to laugh but stopped myself.

I watched the girls who had been laughing and giggling, daring each other into silly antics only an hour before, and realized that this might be just a game but quite a few of them were taking it seriously. I saw Abby take a very pointed deep breath as she stared at Trent, the expansion of her lungs swelling her chest until I was certain her large breasts were going to spill out of the sweetheart neckline of her gown. Unfortunately for her, Trent's attention was on Skip.

Something was odd there, but I let it go as the last of

my competition came down the stairs and settled onto a couch.

"There you have it, ladies and gentlemen, a full cast of beautiful players. Let's learn a little more about each, shall we?" Skip gave us all a wink as someone shouted out the words 'relax for five'.

We all took a deep breath and I watched the green-eyed devil try to make his way over to us. I wanted him to come and say hello. I wanted to see if those eyes were just as spellbinding up close. A producer blocked him as we ladies were all led out of the room.

We'd already been filming for two days, interviews that I knew would be cut up to show whatever the producers wanted to show, reels of us interacting with each other and speculating about the men. Another producer came to us and led us into a dining room where we found our names written on small labels.

I took a seat in mine, close to the man named Jake, and tried not to grin. I might not be into this kind of thing, but Jake was a man unlike any I'd ever seen before. His hair was silky and dark, cut short but I noticed how he kept touching it. He must have cut it recently, and I smiled at the idea of long hair. That would have made the civility of that tuxedo a lie. Something about the man screamed feral, wild, and untamed despite the appearance of being just that. I wanted to growl but smothered it down.

I knew the whole thing was silly and I really, really hated these kinds of shows, but he took my breath away. I just hoped the intelligence I'd seen in those eyes was true. If he was beautiful but stupid my heart would break!

"I think it's Trent, he's the rich one. Look at that smile, it's like a shark that's ready to attack. "That Jake guy is hot, but he just doesn't have that air about him wealthy men should have." I noticed it was the dark-haired beauty, Arabella. We all knew by now she was here only for the fame and the money. She'd made it clear to all of us that when she made her choice we were to back off. But then, why had she set her sights on Jake? Was she playing some game to throw the others off?

I couldn't help but roll my eyes at the thought. She was worried about money and I was worried about intelligence, sheesh! I was a law student, independent, and I didn't believe in true love, not really, yet there I was thinking about how my heart would break if Jake turned out to be as thick as a plank. I took a deep breath and picked up a glass filled with red wine. I took a sip and inhaled slowly. I would not make a fool of myself, I repeated as a mantra in my mind.

And then he was in the room, his beautiful full lips smiling for only me. I knew it was for only me because he didn't take his eyes off me though the others around me perked up and tried to catch his eye.

We all sat down for an elegant dinner, all of us talked excitedly, but I couldn't hold the conversation well. I was too engrossed in looking at Jake to really hold the threads. I glanced at the other two men, both fine examples of manhood, but they didn't have the hold over me Jake had. I watched his fingers as he picked up his wineglass, clean short nails tipped long, strong fingers.

I watched him take the glass to his mouth and caught his eyes once more. His lips pursed as he took a slow sip of wine, our eyes caught in a game I'd never played before. His eyebrow quirked as he set the glass down on the table, his fingers stroking the stem. I felt my breath halt in my chest, the way his fingers stroked the glass sent a not so subtle message to my brain and I felt my eyes go wide.

I looked away, confused. Was this that infamous eye sex game I'd heard so much about?

I sent a quick glance back to his eyes and saw a satisfied smile on his face. That smile changed to one of challenge and I smiled boldly, giving him a look of my own. Two could play that game.

"How are you doing, Laney?" he asked me, his voice a stroke of a finger down my spine. I smothered a shudder of pleasure and looked him in the eye.

"I'm alright, and you?"

Polite chitchat, right. I stroked my own finger up the

stem of my wineglass, far more suggestive than his own move was, even if it was the same thing.

"I'm a bit warm... But I think I like it." He took a strawberry from a plate and bit into it, his lips tight around the fruit.

Damn, why was that so hot? Was it because he stared directly at me as he did it?

I imagined the way he'd look at me as I came near, his light eyes burning just as I straddled his lap.

Down girl, down! I told myself as my cheeks flushed with heat. It was desire that made them burn. I could feel my nostrils flaring as he took another bite, and I knew I was in trouble. I glanced at the fruit platter and saw a variety of berries and slices of orange.

I picked up a slice of orange and bit into half of it. The juices ran down my chin so I had to wipe at them. My tongue darted out to lick away the tangy juice on my lips, and his gaze fastened onto the movement. I hadn't done it to be sensual, just to clean my mouth, but he found it to be just that, all the same. I could see it in the way he stared.

Two could play this teasing game, I decided, and gave him a cocky grin, my eyebrow arched. He was just leaning forward, about to carry on, when Skip came in to draw our attention once more.

"Alright, ladies and gentlemen, I hate to interrupt but

the men have a decision to make. Tonight, three of you will be going home."

There were gasps around the room. We hadn't realized there would be an elimination so quickly. I shot a glance at Jake and saw him give me a subtle wink. I looked back down at my hands once more, somehow reassured.

The other girls chattered together, some sending catty comments to girls they obviously felt threatened by. I sat quietly until the other redhead in the group came and sat with me.

"I think you've caught Jake's eye, you lucky dog." She gave me a wide smile and I gave her one back.

"David seems to like you, Kelly." I'd seen him watching her, their eyes sparking with each glance.

"He's a quiet man, but he loves poetry as much as I do." I heard a hint of hope in her voice. "I've dreamed about my Prince Charming since I was little, my own Lord Byron, to spend long winter nights writing with."

She looked lost in the fantasy so I didn't say anything, though I did think to myself that Lord Byron may have been a romantic poet but his love life left something to be desired.

Skip came back into the room and the titter of female voices ceased. We all waited with baited breath as he held up his hand.

"I will call six names now." He paused as we all set off

gasping once more. "Please follow my instructions as I call your name."

"Arabella, please go the drawing room." She stood, a look of triumph casting a glow over her olive-toned face. She was quite lovely, but also quite the bitch from what I'd seen of her so far. Too confident, too sly, she'd made her own band of friends and shot them a look of triumph as she stood to leave.

"Charlotte, you're to go to the library. No, don't cry my dear, you're far too pretty for that." The young woman in question had immediately burst into tears and ran out of the room to do as Skip requested.

"Amelia, please see your way to the sun room." He stopped speaking as he looked us over. He paused for so long we all started to fidget. I wanted to shout at him to get on with it already!

"Beth." He stopped again to build the drama, and all eyes were on the redhead seated beside me. "Please go to the atrium."

That was four down, two more to go.

"Kelly, please find your way to the terrace."

She shot me a look of confusion but I saw a smile as she stood to leave. Confident her Byron had chosen her then. I waited as she exited, my breath held. Skip glanced at each of us at the table. The room was far too quiet as those of us that remained waited.

"Laney, please see your way to the small ballroom upstairs."

The room filled with words of encouragement for me as the other women realized they were safe and not on the chopping block. I gave a wave of appreciation as I left the room, the long skirt of my dress bunched in my hand so I wouldn't trip. What was I going to find there?

I knew where the room was, I'd seen it earlier and was shocked at how small it was. In my mind, I'd always imagined ballrooms as large open galleries with hardwood floors inlaid with ebony or some other decorative wood. This room was painted completely white from ceiling to floor, and quite small, with only two small windows to allow air in for circulation.

I paused as I came to the closed door to the room. Would Jake be on the other side? Would he turn me down after all of that eye... stuff?

I took a deep breath and pushed the door open before I could change my mind, a cameraman not far behind me filming every moment. It was possible to forget they were there, but not always, and now was one of those times when I was keenly aware that I was being filmed. I wanted to tell him to piss off, but knew I couldn't.

I walked into the white room and my eye was immediately caught by a table with a pink rose sitting atop an envelope.

I went to the table, my hands already shaking. My head was totally in the game as I picked up the envelope.

Breaking the red wax seal, I felt my heart thud back to life as I read the words in calligraphy inside.

"Jake would like to invite you to a breakfast for two. Would you like to accept?" I couldn't stop the smile that spread across my face as I read the missive.

Stupidly, tears stung my eyes and I covered my mouth to try to hide some of my face from the camera. I looked away from the bored-looking man holding the camera and heaved a sigh of relief. I was still in the game.

"You can relax now." A producer called out, their signal to the cameraman to stop filming.

"Of course, I'll accept," I said as I turned to the tall, slim woman in her late forties named Carol. She always looked hungry to me, quarrelsome and angry at the same time and I didn't buy that she was trying to instill trust and assurance in us all. It always put me on edge.

"Good, you'd be eliminated in the next round if you'd refused." Her words shocked me but I didn't let her see that. "Go to bed, we have all we need for now."

I left the room a bit deflated. Did her words mean the game was already rigged? How could she assure me I'd be eliminated if the men barely even knew us yet? I pushed the thoughts aside and concentrated on not tripping as the sound of my feet on the hardwood floors reverberated through the hall.

Jake wanted to spend private time with me, but the coldness of the producer reminded me that my emotions and actions were just a product she needed in order to sell the show. I washed my face and took out the contacts the show-runners insisted I wear. I went to bed that night, three other girls in twin beds around me constantly breaking the quiet, with a smile on my face despite the producer. I might not have come into this game looking for love and I really thought I'd be the first to be eliminated, but I was still here and now that I'd seen Jake and had a date with him in the morning, well, I wanted to keep it that way.

CHAPTER FOUR

JAKE

I woke up early and insisted on getting some work done over a cup of coffee. The producers had balked and glared at my stipulations but when I threatened them with my departure they soon changed their tune. They still limited my use of the phone and the Internet, but my business was my priority and I wouldn't let them threaten it.

My hand went to my hair, an old habit I still couldn't break despite the cut, as a crew of people came into the large bedroom and began to dress a table with fine china, a linen tablecloth with an autumn theme, and spread out jams and butters. They didn't even ask to come in, but they didn't even acknowledge my existence, so I guess my privacy wasn't an issue.

I'd showered and dressed while the camera crew set up, and now we waited for the lady of the hour to come take her place. I tapped nervously at the table top, shifting in my dark blue jeans, an old pair that fit me just right, with a wheat brown knit sweater keeping out the chill in the room.

I had quite a few dates to get through in the coming days, and it wasn't going to take nearly as long as I thought if we were each going to eliminate three at one time. I didn't care about the other girls. Laney's smile and her kind eyes had already caught my attention. This "date" was just a formality as far as I was concerned.

"Look, Jake, you obviously like Laney, but we really need you to set up something with Arabella. She's our main focus for the next few segments, so we need you to give her some time, okay? Trent and David are playing ball, we need you to get on board with this." A woman I knew to be a producer came into the room, her blasé manner putting me on edge. I was unsure if her name was actually Carol, so I avoided using it.

"I thought the point of the game was for us to choose who we wanted, and they have to figure out which of us is the billionaire. It would be nice to know I'm wanted for something other than my money." I gave the woman a wave of my hand, a dismissal I had never used before but the woman put me on edge.

"Oh, like that, are we?" Her red brow pointed, a sign of irritation she seemed to think would bring me into line. Her garish red hair was piled onto her head in an artfully haphazard way that was meant to convey care-lessness, but with the amount of hairspray she had in it, you knew it was by design. "You have read the contract, right?"

"I have, yes." I bristled and wondered if I'd missed something but one of the other producers came in to tell everybody to get out but me and the cameraman, Laney was on her way. The conversation ended, but Carol gave me a side-eyed glance that I knew meant I needed to do as she dictated.

A man came in with a cue card and a single camera on a tripod.

"We just need a few minutes of 'diary film', please," he said, yet another of those that didn't even bother to look at me.

I sat down in the chair he indicated and waited.

"Why did you choose Laney?" he asked, without even warming me up first.

"Because she seems so sweet and down to earth. I saw her walking down those stairs and she just seemed... I don't know, real, I guess."

"Right," he said without inflection. "Why not one of the others? This is your first date after all, why not one of the more fun ones?"

"Laney looks like she's intelligent, fun, and full of life. What do you mean?"

"Maybe I should have been blunt. Why not one of the

sexier ones that might get their clothes off for the camera?" He looked up now, his gaze nailing me to the chair.

Apparently, I'd done something wrong.

"Because I can get sex anywhere. I'm here to find a wife, aren't I? The woman I can spend the rest of my life with? Laney looks like that kind of a woman."

"Okay. That's all. See you next time."

The man left then, and I was glad to see the back of him. What stupid questions. Yeah, you can be blatantly sexy, you can put everything you have on display, but to be able to take part in erotic play, to be able to seduce with your eyes and your brain? Yeah, Laney was at the very top of my list.

I'd nearly jumped out of my chair when she bit into the orange slice. She'd looked so confused, uncertain, as we'd first started to play, but when she caught on, her eyes had lit up and she'd followed my lead. Not afraid of sex, smart, and beautiful. Why would I choose anyone else?

With a sigh of frustration, I stood. I wanted to be alone with her, I wanted to touch her and taste her, but I knew this had to go slow. There were cameras everywhere, and I didn't want to rush anything with her. She was more than just a fuck and a goodbye, this one. She was worth getting to know.

As soon as Laney came into the room and I saw how

her eyes were bright and her cheeks were bare of makeup, the frustration fled. She wore a pair of black velour pants and a white cable-knit sweater with a low neckline. Comfy but still sexy, I decided. Just like the woman wearing them.

"Hi." I took her hand with the simple greeting and led her to the chair directly across from me. "How are you today?"

"Fine. Nervous." She gave me a wobbly smile that soon firmed into a grin as she took her seat, brushing back a stray lock of her hair. "Those cameras are everywhere!"

I smiled at her conspiratorially. "Evil, aren't they?"

"Very." She breathed the word as she picked up a menu at the plate beside her.

"Did you sleep alright?" I was making small talk, my own nerves getting the better of me with her in front of me.

I knew she was the reason my tongue felt tied, and my legs were jiggling almost involuntarily. I'd never reacted to a woman quite like I did to Laney, and I'd barely held a conversation with her that could be called anything but small talk. Yet, here I was, wanting to stroke those long delicate artist's fingers. I wasn't sure if she was an artist but she should have been with fingers like that. Slim and elegant, they were tipped with clear nail polish that brought a sheen to the not so long but not too short nails.

My gaze traveled up the length of her arm and I appreciated how smooth her skin looked, soft and silky. My gaze moved on as she spoke, and she told me about the intricacies of sleeping with three other women in the same room. Her throat was just as elegant as the rest of her, made to cradle my head perfectly. And her mouth…

Peach-tinted lips moved, the flash of white teeth with a slight crook to the front two caught my eye. Her front bicuspid overlapped the other one just slightly, a fault I found endearing. And then I was looking at her smiling eyes.

"So you like wearing pink yoga pants and bows in your hair, do you?" She looked pleased with herself and I knew I'd been caught.

"Pardon?" I blinked and knew I'd been caught as I stared at her. I'd been too caught up in memorizing every inch of her I could spot to hear exactly what she'd said or asked.

"You started to say "mmm" to everything. So I asked if you liked wearing yoga pants and hair bows and you nodded and murmured "mmm", so there you go. Own it, buddy, you like pink yoga pants."

"Maybe on you, Laney, but never on me." The playfully spoken words were out before I could draw them back and I felt something unusual happen, a burn in my cheeks I haven't felt since I was an awkward teenager.

"It's alright, I was only teasing you." She reached out for my hand, a move that seemed to surprise even her, but I took her hand in mine gratefully.

"I don't seem to be myself, either." Don't get me wrong, I'm no virgin, I've had my share of girlfriends and affairs, but something about Laney returned me to the sixteen-year-old I used to be.

I wasn't very cool back then. I was overweight, a computer nerd seeing the world in computer languages I wanted to invent, dreaming of building my own empire. I started to exercise when I went to college at seventeen, and I built a physique that many envied. I'd also learned a lot about what women want and how to satisfy them. I'd come into this a little jaded and a whole lot of cynical; Laney changed all of that.

"What do you want?" She gave me a calm smile and my pulse thudded in my neck. Her effect on me was immediate.

"I'd love nothing more than to take you out on that beach and walk for miles with you." I waved in the general direction of where I thought the beach was in relation to the house.

With a laugh, she held up the menu. "I meant for breakfast?"

"I, uh, well, I guess I should look first." My cheeks were burning again, I just knew it.

She leaned back as she looked over the menu once more and I couldn't help but notice the way the heavy cotton of her sweater made the neckline fall open. I could see the curve of generous breasts and a cleavage made for, well, things that good boys didn't think about.

I'd never said I was an angel though, had I? I wanted to run my finger down that scented valley, to explore those soft globes with my hands, my tongue, and all the things that would make her frantic for more. I needed to stop my train of thought because soon standing up without embarrassment would be impossible.

We moved through breakfast, and she told me about her life, her roommate, her goals, and I was quite impressed. A young woman with drive. She pushed for what she wanted and took it. That was a strong pull for me.

I'd been lucky and had attended college at an early age on a full scholarship, and some would say money was just drawn to me. I rarely touched a project that didn't succeed, in fact, I've never had one fail. Laney, on the other hand, struggled for what she had, even if she did have help from her parents on occasion. She didn't complain, though, she just gave me the facts. I really admired that.

I'd almost forgotten the cameras, she put me at ease

so well, but I saw them when we stood to go for that walk I suggested.

"Carol says you have twenty minutes, then there are other things to do. Other choices to make." He looked at me with an apology and I couldn't be mad at him.

"Fine. Tell her we'll be back soon enough." I put my hand in the small of Laney's back and we moved through the house, the heels of her boots clicking on the hardwood floors.

We were soon in the fresh air. A slight breeze blew her long hair around her face. She really took my breath away.

"So, what do you, well... I suppose you can't answer that. What do you do for fun?"

I knew she'd been about to ask what I did for a living, but the girls weren't supposed to outright ask.

"I don't have a lot of time for fun, really." Shit, would that give it away? I wondered as she looked at me sharply. "There's a lot of work involved in what I do, and well, there isn't much down time. If I do have any, I'm usually helping my grandmother with her house."

Yeah, that sounded better than me telling her I live in my Gran's basement, and when I'm not working on projects I'm fixing the leaking roof or nailing down carpet that she refused to let me replace but came loose from the floor regularly. She wanted to keep the house the way it was when my grandfather was alive, and I wasn't going to force her to change it.

"That's very kind of you." She glanced at me as we avoided the surf. It wasn't the time of year for dances in the surf.

"It's what a grandchild should do for someone who loves them, right?" I looked off into the distance, thinking of the blue eyes of my grandmother. More to me than a grandmother, she'd filled two roles since my parents died, and I could never repay that with money.

I'd been an awkward, subdued thirteen-year-old after they died in a house fire that took their lives but spared me. She'd done her best to make life normal for me as I'd eaten my way through my grief. She'd been the one that bought me a gym membership when I went off to college. I'd slowly started to be able to control the memory of flames and my parents' screams and moved on with life. Grief still plagued me, but not as often as it had in the beginning.

"I suppose so. Both sets of my grandparents are gone now, I never really knew what that was like." She sounded wistful and I knew what she was feeling. That longing for something that you aren't quite sure is real.

"She's a star. Ooof!" She'd tumbled over a hidden piece of driftwood and I caught her before she fell. Her body fell against mine and awareness singed through us both, sparking like static electricity. "You're beautiful."

I felt the words breathe over my lips before I could stop them and she gave me a happy smile. I couldn't help what I did next, it just happened, before I even knew I intended to do it.

One minute I was looking into her eyes, the next, her lips were beneath mine, stirring a longing I'd never felt before. The soft flesh of her mouth moved beneath mine, shy, but exploring, and I tasted the cinnamon of her French toast in the corner of her smile.

"You taste beautiful, too," I told her as she pulled away, a secret smile of delight on her face. Her eyes burned with a desire to explore further, a desire I felt keenly myself, but the sight of Carol, furious and tearing through the sand in our direction, halted that desire.

"What did I say to you?" She called out as she came near. "You have to follow our instructions, or this is not going to work!"

"That's fine by me." Again with the impulsive tongue. I was going to have to learn to control it.

She stared at me, her lips moving but not forming words. "I need to see you in the office." Her words were cold and without emotion when she finally spoke.

She stormed off, her straight back and stiff neck told me she expected me to follow but I hesitated.

"I really like you, Laney. Don't lose faith, alright?"

I knew Carol was trying to push me toward this Arabella, she'd mentioned her incessantly, but I wasn't interested. I also knew Carol was about to drop a bomb on me, I'd seen it in the cold anger in her eyes.

Laney gave me a gentle smile and I left her in the sand, an assistant helping her to navigate around the beach in her boots.

This was not going to end well for me, Carol's demeanor screamed it at me as she walked away. I just hope it didn't ruin the start to what I knew could be something beautiful. I could still taste Laney on my lips, and my hands went to brush against them, remembering how much I'd wanted to take it further. I remembered how hard I'd grown looking at her this morning as I fantasized about her. This was more than just desire though, I knew that the same as I knew my own name. Laney might really be the one.

CHAPTER FIVE

LANEY

"And that's when I knew that the frat boy life was for me." Trent produced a toothy, confident smile that I could all but hear the cameras zooming in on as he finished his tale of hazing freshmen as the women around him tittered into their pretty hands.

I tried to hide the rolling of my eyes by looking away to take a sip of my apple juice as he droned on, his voice laced with a hint of an English accent that made me think he was one big fake.

I'd quickly grown tired of the constant supply of alcohol. I'm not much of a drinker after all and asked for water. The producers had balked, wanting to show the audience a glamorous life filled with good wine, so they'd watered down apple juice to give to me. I sipped at it as voices filled the dining room, noise that only served to put me on edge.

Three days of backbiting behind closed doors, the constant presence of the cameras, two fistfights between some of the women, and frustration at being treated like a child had me ready to give them all the finger and head back home. But the reason I was fighting so hard to stay in the game soon walked into the candlelit dining room. I forgot about the snide comments about me being stuck up, coming from women who didn't realize I hated the constant chatter and noise, the constant stress of never being alone as soon as Jake walked into the room.

I watched him, noting the tenseness of his jaw, the way his shoulders stretched the material of his black button up shirt in just the right way.

I thought so, I decided as I watched him. There was going to be an elimination tonight. It had been three days, it was time to shake us all up again.

The guys weren't supposed to show favoritism, but Jake had made it clear from day one that I was the only woman he was really interested in. Even if Arabella did seem to think she had the whole contest bagged. I glanced at the dark-eyed beauty, her perfect features schooled into the perfect expression of preoccupation. It made her look mysterious.

I looked away from her and back to Jake. Whenever we were in the same room we were drawn to each other, always aware of the other. I found it disquieting, but also very thrilling. I've never felt like this about anyone before. Carol, the mad producer, came into the room and steered Jake towards Arabella by blocking his path. I didn't understand why that woman was so keen on Arabella and Jake getting together, but I knew that's what she was doing.

Arabella snagged her chance to sink her claws into the sleeve of Jake's shirt to hold him still as she turned on a sexy smile and eased up to him. "Hey, baby, you look good enough to eat tonight."

I could tell from her tone she was trying to be sexy, and in any other situation she would have been, but all I heard was desperation. I knew I was being a bit petty, but I couldn't help it. The woman set me on edge. I didn't feel threatened by her, Jake's interest in me was fairly obvious to everyone but Arabella and Carol, but her using her sexuality to get what she wanted made my skin crawl.

"I think I'd be a bit tough," he said in a tone that suggested anything but enthusiasm, but her fingers still clung to his sleeve.

"I bet I could relax those muscles of yours."

I nearly barfed when I heard her say that. I reached for the bottle of white wine on the table. I needed at least one drink to get me through this farce.

"I dare say you could, Arabella. You could probably clear my pipes without having to call a plumber as well, but I don't have time for this right now." His eyes were searching for me and soon found me.

"Is that a clue?" She looked put off, her artificially plumped top lip curled so much a line of red lipstick appeared just below her nose.

She thought he was giving her inside information. He wasn't paying attention, though, because he came to me, his fingers taking my hand as he quickly whispered to me.

"You're safe, don't panic." He gave me a wink before he stepped back.

"But the other guys could vote me out." I looked at him, my only concern written on my face clearly.

"It's okay." He mouthed with a slight shake of his head, his smile in place as always when I saw him. Damn, why was that so sexy? "I have to go mingle, Carol will kill me if I don't. I'm dying to kiss you. I'll see you later."

I grinned at that part somewhere in the middle. I wanted to kiss him too. Not in some schoolgirl way, but in the hot way he kissed me in my dreams, with our bodies straining to get closer and barely able to breathe. I'd wake up flustered and still hot. I'd find myself watching him, remembering the way he moved in the dreams, the skillful way he touched me. With a quiet groan of frustration, I turned away and forced myself to think about something else.

I considered the likelihood that Jake was the billion-aire, more for the mysterious puzzling quality of it than real curiosity. I knew he liked computer games, but he kept himself fit. A computer nerd wouldn't have the kind of muscle tone Jake had, surely? A teacher then? He was patient, kind, and listened to others when they spoke to him. He also had incredible eyes that were sometimes filled with sadness and I wanted the chance to understand why. I also wanted to know what it felt like to run my fingers through his hair.

Maybe Trent was the rich guy. I couldn't see the loud, obnoxious man as a teacher, not with his attitude about bullying others. I'd spoken with him a few times, but I kept the brash blond at a distance every time. He just didn't do anything for me.

David, then? Kelly's pick was quiet, sweet, and very poetic. I couldn't see him as a plumber, not at all. Not with those polished nails. That thought left me even more confused though. That meant Jake would have to be the plumber, but he didn't seem the kind of guy that would find that job fulfilling and if there was anything I'd figured out about Jake so far, it was that he was happy where he was in life. It was hands-on and computer games were hands-on, maybe that was it.

It didn't really matter to me. A plumber, teacher, or a rich man: they all had jobs that meant they could take care of themselves. I still didn't know how this was all going to end, or what the producers had in store for us. So far, we'd had "dates" that had left me cringing but I participated as I was supposed to.

One date had us all writing our pet peeves down on a piece of paper and the men had to figure out which they belonged to. Jake found mine, of course. We had picnics on the beach, walks through the forest, bike rides around the estate which was basically half of the island, and a day of sports where we tossed around a Frisbee, played softball and volleyball, all in the obligatory outfits provided by the show.

Another day we had to choose a movie for a movie date. I found it all laughable, because these dates involved six women and three men. How were we supposed to make a decision about the rest of our lives based on less than two weeks of interaction that wasn't private? I had to laugh at myself as Jake's eyes found me across the room once more. I already knew I wanted to get to know the man better, spend some real time with him.

"I swear you two are gross!" Kelly said as she sat down and poured herself a glass of wine. "I'm going to have to write a poem about it."

A squeeze of her hand over mine on the table let me know she was teasing.

"As if you and David are any different!" I found the man talking with a pretty blonde, his expression bored as he glanced longingly at Kelly before looking back at the woman who talked with her hands incessantly.

"We are! We're less obvious than you two." She gave a snort through her nose then blushed. "He kissed me earlier. An amazing kiss that literally curled my toes!"

She had on one of those dreamy smiles of pure happiness. At least the producers were leaving them alone. That made me wonder if Jake really was the rich one, the seeming determination to force him and Arabella together, but not the other men with other women, was telling.

"Oh my, that's serious!" I couldn't imagine the quiet, respectful man daring to kiss Kelly.

She was vivacious, beautiful, and really very interesting, though she tended to draw more out of you than you did out of her. She was curious about people and she'd have made a great journalist if she hadn't been so set on poetry. She was good at that too, I'd seen some of what she'd written since she'd been here, and the epic poems were really good.

"He asked me..." She went quiet and looked around for a moment before she turned back to me. "He asked me if I'd see him when this is all over."

"Isn't that the point of the choice? You get to decide that?" I looked at her confused.

"Well, there are whisperings that the producers are trying to force matches." She gave a quiet nod to

Arabella and to Jake. "He heard Carol telling the other producers that Jake needed to stop with you because it was going to kill their ratings."

"What?" I looked at her aghast, and more than a little angry. "What, I'm not some dark-haired, sloe-eyed beauty, so they think viewers will hate me? Have they even paid attention to her personality? Viewers are going to hate her!"

I bent closer to Kelly as she looked around again to make sure we wouldn't be overheard. "You have to be careful, Laney. They really mean business and you could be sent home tonight."

"But Jake said—"

"I think Carol might just put your name in to be voted off, no matter what the men have agreed."

"That evil bitch!"

"I think you should remember." She patted my head again as Skip came in and she spoke more quickly. "This will end and whatever happens after that, there won't be a Carol or an Arabella to get in the way."

I clenched my fingers this time and breathed deeply as I ran my tongue over my back teeth, lost in thought. Kelly was right, anything could happen on this stupid show. Did I even know enough about Jake to trust him? To trust that he wouldn't take what Arabella so openly, eagerly, offered? I saw how she kept looking at him, her hands constantly smoothing down the line of the costumes we wore tonight.

Simple, figure-hugging silk sleeveless knee-length dresses, this time in soft metallic tones. Hers was in a deep shade of gold, while mine was copper. Where hers showed off an hourglass figure and a tight bottom, mine showed off a more plump but toned figure. At least my boobs are bigger than hers, I thought snidely before I chided myself.

"I really hate this place, you know?" I said to Kelly, wrapping my arms over my chest, anxiety making me queasy.

"It's a lot harder on you than it is on me, that's for sure. I'd be frantic if I were you." For a moment, I had to wonder if Kelly was playing a role, if she was trying to make me nervous, but her eyes were clear of guile, and I was fairly certain I could trust her. What would she gain through sabotage?

In a paranoid moment, I thought maybe Carol had offered her something to make me nervous, but I saw that for what it was. Paranoia, plain and simple. This place, where we were so secluded from the real world, where we couldn't talk to our family or friends, or escape to a quiet place as I'd like to do, was bound to breed paranoia.

The only real private moments we got was if the men chose us for a private date. Jake had chosen me for breakfast at the beginning, David had chosen Kelly for lunch yesterday, and Trent chose Arabella for dinner last night. The cycle would start over once this elimination was done.

"Laney, video diary time," said the man I'd become accustomed to asking me personal questions I'd usually punch somebody for. Well, maybe not punch but certainly wouldn't answer.

"Fine."

I went into a small room where he directed me to a chair. As usual, he went straight for the jugular.

"Do you think you'll be eliminated tonight?" He was watching the camera, not me.

I smiled and shook my head. "Not really. I think Jake and I are forming a real bond. Something that a few people around here don't seem to like."

"Do you think Jake will pick Arabella for a private date this time?" He seemed to want to rile me.

"Maybe, but he has to pick somebody else this time, doesn't he? He can't pick me twice." I remained calm and stared into the camera.

"Who do you think should be eliminated tonight?" He looked at me with a slight spark of glee and I knew he wanted me to fall into a trap.

"I don't know, really. There are some who should go, and others that clearly aren't standing out, but it's not my decision, is it?" Oh yeah, attorney deflection at its best!

"Fine, that's all for now then." He shooed me out of the room and I'd only just settled back into my place beside Kelly when Skip came in.

"Ladies and gentlemen, if I could have your attention, please. The time has come. Gentlemen, if you'll follow me, please." Skip broke into the conversations going on around us and everyone turned silently, staring at the man grinning in glee as we waited for the world to crumble.

CHAPTER SIX

JAKE

"I don't care what your plan is, you can fuck right off with it." I glared at the clownish woman with her garish hair and her mean eyes and turned to face the window. The sun was long set but I could still see crashing waves in the moonlight, off in the distance. I would much rather be out there with Laney than stuck in here with Carol. "If you don't like it, I'd be more than happy to leave."

"Fine, Jake, you win this time," the grouchy woman said with a sigh. "But we'll see how long it lasts."

I didn't turn as she left the large office we were using to discuss eliminations. "The choice is made then, gentlemen?"

Skip looked at us all and then turned. "Good. Follow me."

We followed the man through the hallway and back

down to the dining room. The ladies had waited for over an hour as I argued against eliminating Laney. Trent and Carol had been all for it. David and I both stood our ground until they relented.

"Ladies, please, I need your attention. Tonight, we will be eliminating four of you." The room filled with gasps as the ladies realized that we were getting close to the end of this game.

If four were eliminated, that would leave five to choose from and the viewers would be going wild. The program was supposed to run throughout the month of December and conclude on Christmas Eve. I still had no idea how they were going to do it, but I knew they'd want something spectacular.

We men stood behind Skip, waiting for the furor to calm.

"When I call your name, please go to your room and pack your bags. You'll be leaving the island immediately." Skip pursed his lips together, as though he'd tasted something awful, and took a deep breath.

"Abby, Samantha, Edina, and Sally, you have all been eliminated by our bachelors. You may go." Skip said the names in staccato fashion, as though he were pulling the sticky bandage from a sensitive wound. He gave the camera a look that would surely be interpreted as his heart breaking, but I knew the man was really just after a drink.

The sounds of sobbing and goodbyes broke the silence his words left, while we men stood there like lumps. I thought there was quite a bit wrong with this program, quite a bit, but I wasn't putting it together. To me it seemed almost amateurish, not well thought out, but I wasn't the one paying for it, so I kept my thoughts to myself. Let them work out why the show would do poorly after it had aired.

I felt almost ashamed of myself as one woman walked past, Edina I think, her mascara running down her face as tears continued to spill from her eyes. I'd been struck by the brutality of the show from the beginning, but that look of defeat was terrible to witness. The cynical side of me said she'd not been attached to any of us men, that she was either crying because she'd failed and had been eliminated or because she thought she'd lost her chance at a rich lifestyle. Then, I thought that maybe she was just sad to leave the friends she'd made.

I wished Gran had never signed me up for the show. Lying that wasn't really lying, our lives controlled by morons, and girls walking away crying. Brutal stuff that wasn't my normal style. I hated it, really. I felt as helpless now to change my future as I did when I first learned my parents hadn't made it out of the fire.

I tried to push the thought away. My teeth clenched together even though I knew I must look rather grim, but the pain came through anyway. I sought out Laney's eyes and saw how calm she was, how she had eyes only for me, and a smile that made me think only of sex. I wanted to hold her, to lose myself in her, if only we could find some time alone!

"Ladies, there are only five of you left. Make your moves wisely." Skip spoke to the ladies with the voice of a wise old man imparting great knowledge and I had to fight to keep my eyes from rolling. "Gentlemen, you have five minutes to speak with the ladies before we must separate you again."

I headed straight for Laney, I wanted to tell her to meet me in the ballroom later, once the lights had all gone out. Carol tried to block me, but I walked past her with speed, not letting her stand in my way this time. I took Laney's hands, whispered to her quickly, and waited until she'd given me a look of understanding. I'd see her later, I didn't care where Carol dragged me off to now.

"Jake, why do I keep finding you around Miss Plain Jane here? Come here, baby, let me show you how a real woman shows her appreciation." With that Arabella planted a kiss on me designed to knock my socks off. Her full lips, passionate tongue play, and wandering hands might have done it if her touch didn't make me cringe.

I gently pushed her away, wiping at my mouth furiously as I grabbed a discarded glass of wine to wash her taste away. She stood there with a look of self-satisfaction on her face, but it slipped a little when I wiped my tongue with a napkin.

"What have you been eating?" I asked as Skip called out for the men to leave.

Carol might have convinced Arabella I was the one for her, but I'd made it clear—I hoped—that I wasn't interested. Normally I would be appalled at such rude behavior, but Arabella acted like she already owned me and I wanted her to know it wasn't true.

I went back to my room and showered. I didn't know what the night had in store, but I wanted that woman's taste and touch washed away from me before I went anywhere near Laney.

I CREPT along the dark hallway, one ear trained to listen for other footsteps as I headed for the ballroom just after midnight. I didn't know if Laney would show or not, but I hoped she would. I let myself into the room and, with only socks on my feet, I found my way to a window and opened a curtain to allow the moonlight in.

I brought two ladderback chairs to the window, pulled out a bottle of water and two plastic cups from the stash in my room, and passed the time by reading an eBook on my phone. I didn't have too long to wait before the door cracked and a face whitened by moonlight peeked in.

I stood and couldn't help but grin when I saw her feet in white cotton socks. I knew she was a smart girl. I liked the sage green flannel pajamas she had on too, mainly because they had buttons. I have a thing about buttons, well, opening them. Especially when Laney is the one with the buttons to open.

She came to me without a word, her fingers settled over my lips until she stood on tiptoe and brought my face down to hers. In an instant I needed her, I wanted her, and I pulled her close, our tongues tracing around each other sinuously. I moved back, dragging us both to the wall so I could lean back as she pressed her softness into me.

I couldn't hold back a groan of pleasure as she pressed her lower abdomen into me, I was already on fire for her and my hands tried to pull her impossibly tighter to me. I wanted to be a part of her, inside of her, surrounding her.

Our lips joined in a frenzied dance, the long wait making it impossible to go slow. I popped the buttons of her pajamas with nimble fingers, needing to feel the silken warmth of her flesh in my palms. I found her breasts bare and eager to fill my hands, and I knew the tips had to ache they were so tight. I broke the kiss and dipped my head down, pulling her up just enough to get her nipple between my teeth.

I heard her hiss in a breath as her fingers dived into my hair, her back arched to press her breast deeper into the wet heat I offered her. I sucked at the nipple until her hips started to dance against me, and then I found the other nipple, only to tease her into a groaning sob of pleasure. Her fingers played over my head for a moment and I wished I hadn't cut off my hair. It would feel so good to have my hair come down around my shoulders as her fingers wound into the tresses. It didn't seem to matter though, as her fingers dove into what was left. Her purr of delight made me grin. Women loved my hair, short or long.

My teeth scraped at the delicate flesh for a moment longer, my fingers pinching the other in just the right way, before I swiped at both with my tongue. I wanted to bury myself in Laney, I wanted to lose myself in her velvet walls, but first, I wanted to hear her come.

She started to protest as I slid down her body, pushing the softness of her pants away as I did so, but I soothed her.

"Shh. Let me taste you, Laney. I've dreamed about what you taste like, and I want to know if I was right." I scattered light kisses along her stomach, further down, just below her belly button, my fingers brushed the spaces I'd missed until her pants were gone. I turned her, pushed her against the wall, and spread her thighs apart as I sank to my knees before her.

"What are you doing to me, Jake?" She whispered raggedly, her body already yearning towards me. Her body knew what it wanted, even if she didn't.

"Making you mine." With that, I grasped at her bottom with both hands and tilted her slick center into my mouth.

I spread her nether lips with my tongue, tasted her briefly, and closed my eyes in pleasure as her delicate taste filled my senses. She was so very good.

Her fingers wound into my hair once more as her breath caught in her chest. I heard her panting as my tongue split her open, but when I found her clit and sucked it into my mouth, she cried out my name. That's what I wanted, that's what I needed, to hear Laney sobbing my name out in a moan of pure pleasure.

I was rock hard in my pants, painfully hard, but Laney needed to come and come she would before I even thought about my own relief.

I pressed her abdomen back into the wall, knowing that the tilt would put pressure on her inner walls. Just as I heard her gasping, I used that same hand to seek out her heated core and pressed into her. Deep and slow, I explored her with my fingers and my mouth, as I savored the delicate tightness of her, the way she clenched around my finger with each new penetration of my finger.

I glanced up and saw a vision of raw desire in the moonlight, Laney's face frozen in concentration as she drew near to ultimate pleasure. I almost stopped, I almost stood to plunge myself into her, but I held onto my self-control. I used my tongue to dart at her taut clit, and her hips danced once more, dancing to my tune as I stroked her with my finger.

She mewled helplessly, wanting more, wanting what was just out of reach, until I felt the first fluttering spasm of her walls contracting in pure surrender. I drank her in as she came apart, her abdomen fluttering as my practiced tongue pushed her higher. She gulped in air as the waves passed through her body, her back arched, and I had to hang on to keep my tongue centered on her.

Laney's ecstasy only made me impossibly harder, and I wanted to bury myself in her desperately, but she wasn't done. I've made women come before, I've seen some beautiful sights, but Laney's pleasure went on and on, she became little more than the embodiment of pleasure as I stroked her higher.

I heard a sound of satisfaction and realized it had rumbled out of my own chest as she finally started to come down. Laney had gone off like a volcano, but now she was coming down. Her juices covered my face, her scent filled my head, and I knew I would never be able to get her out of my mind.

I swiped at my mouth as I stood and placed one hand against the wall as I leaned into her.

"That was beautiful," I said as I looked down at her. Her eyes were dazed and I knew she wanted to sink to the floor. My hand on her waist held her up, and visions of those long, muscled thighs wrapped around me made me groan in pain.

"That was... wow, that was amazing."

She was still catching her breath and I let my forehead fall to hers so that we could look at each other directly.

"You know we're fucked, right? At least until this show is over and I can get you in my own bed." I made a mental note to tell my personal assistant to find a nice tiny apartment somewhere near where Gran lived.

"Where do you live?" She asked, as if only then realizing we might live in different states.

I knew I couldn't tell her exactly where I lived, it was against the rules, but I could tell her the state. "South Carolina, the same as you. It's not that big, we won't be far apart."

I wanted to keep talking, I wanted to tell her everything there was to know about me, but I also wanted to hear her gasping my name again, desperately.

I was about to suggest we find somewhere more suitable to sit when I heard voices outside.

"They have to be here somewhere. Find them."

Carol and her meddling assistants! Fuck!

"Hurry, get your pants on."

"But you..." Her voice trailed off as the knob on the door rattled.

I froze because I couldn't remember if Laney had locked the door or not. I turned to hide her body as the knob rattled once more.

CHAPTER SEVEN

LANEY

A night full of steamy dreams interspersed with memories of my fingers wound in Jake's hair ended when somebody slammed the door to my room. I woke up the next morning with my hair glued to my face, my thighs aching pleasantly, with a desperate need for a shower, but I was still smiling. I smiled through the long wait for a bathroom to be empty so I could have that much-needed shower. I smiled as I soaped up my body, loving the slickness as I scrubbed with my washcloth. I could remember exactly every move Jake had made.

I sighed deeply as I leaned back in the stall, remembering how his strong hands had held me to his face. I sighed loudly when I remembered the way his tongue ran up my folds and shivered against the wall. I closed my eyes, letting the memories take me away. That is until somebody walked in and interrupted me by dropping something loudly.

Even then I smiled, because I could remember the way Jake's lips had brushed against my hairline just in front of my ear as he'd whispered good night to me. The way his voice rumbled in my ear and his hair stroked against my cheek sent a shiver down my spine even then.

I smiled through Carol's glares and suspicious glances during breakfast. The door had been locked so she hadn't been able to confront us. She'd knocked for several minutes before she'd growled and stomped off. Jake and I had both dressed quickly when we realized the door was locked, but I suspected she was waiting for us just outside and stopped him from leaving straight away.

He'd pulled me to the door, his lips finding mine in the darkness. I'd inhaled his scent, a masculine cologne that left traces on my skin. I ran my fingers along his jaw as he kissed me, wanting to gather his scent so I could smell him later. Our breathing was ragged again by the time he pulled away.

"I feel like I'm killing myself by doing this, Laney, but we have to go to our rooms. We'll be in for a shitload of whining if Carol catches us. I don't really care what she has to say to me, but I know she gives you a hard time. I would drag you to my bed, strip you down, and fuck you until the sheets were soaked with your wetness. But I'd rather not do it here anyway. There are probably cameras." He'd kissed me once more. His body was pressed against mine, his hardness against my softness a draw I couldn't resist.

My hands went to his tight, round ass so I could pull him tighter against me. I squeezed it and he groaned into the top of my head.

"We have to stop, Laney. Come on, please. I don't want my first time with you to be a quick fuck against the door. I want a bed and hours to hear you purr."

I sighed with contentment and let him pull away. Who could turn that down?

We'd gone back to our rooms separately and, even though I'd thought I wouldn't be able to sleep for hours, I'd dropped off right away. Now, showered, dressed, and fed, I was ready to see what the day brought.

My smile didn't waver as the day's agenda was passed out. I even smiled when I read that I was expected to go on "dates" with Trent and David.

Nothing could take that smile away, not after what had happened with Jake. The man had made my toes literally curl against the floor. His words after, the way he sighed with deep longing as we finally parted, still made something tight take over my torso until I wanted to hug it away. I'd never felt like this, not even when I was a teenager and I'd had a crush on the lead male for the senior play my freshman year. The blond teenage god had all but made me screech with joy when he'd chosen me to play the lead female role.

Dark clouds and wet grass hadn't dimmed my smile, nor had Arabella's snide glances. In fact, my smile broadened when she slipped on a pile of wet leaves as she went to a car for her "date" and ended up soaking wet. The chill in the air would make her day even more miserable I knew.

I stopped smiling when I realized why I was being sent to the other side of the island for these dates when not a single other woman had come along. It started when Carol cornered me at the cozy little cabin that had been set up for a lunch date with Trent.

I didn't really like the man. He was overbearing, rude, and was always making me cringe with tales of exploits I didn't think were worth bragging about. He never seemed to notice, and he'd just plow right on with his tale. I'd stood up and walked away quite a few times but he still hadn't quite caught on.

Now, Carol stood at the cabin door, her face grim. She held the door open for me and I walked in. I heard the lock click and turned to look at her confused. The room was empty. Where was Trent? I was about to ask when she held up a hand.

"Did you forget we have cameras all over the house? We might not have been able to see what you and Jake were doing last night in the ballroom, Laney, but we know you were in there. You have to stop this nonsense, you're going to ruin the show!" She looked at me with anger burning in her eyes.

"I can't help how I feel…" I started but she interrupted me with a sour look on her face.

"Feelings? *Feelings?* Is that all you can think about? Are you really that stupid, girl? This show isn't about virginal feelings and swooning over a gallant prince, it's about photo opportunities, it's about publicity for the producers and the channel. It's about money, and you are about to ruin it for us all with your schoolgirl feelings! I mean, you're not even that photogenic!"

I wasn't a virgin, and far from a schoolgirl, so I took her words as an insult, as I'm certain they were meant to be. And what was that part about not being photogenic? I might not be Miss America, but I certainly wasn't ugly.

"Now look, Carol—"

"No, you listen to me, missy." She huffed a bit and blew her long bangs out of her eyes. "I have a lot of shit to get done today. I don't have time to go chasing after two idiots who think they're in love. You will leave Jake alone, you'll have your date with Trent and David, and that's that. Understood?"

I didn't really give a toss what she thought, but at that point, I knew the game was almost over. I could wait a few more days. Carol might be a pain in my butt, but it was almost done and I felt like I owed it to Kelly not to ruin the rest of the show. Besides, the world would see Arabella as the winner if I left now, wouldn't they? I thought all of this as Carol pushed past me on her way to the door.

"Just keep your legs closed, and do as you're told. Arabella is going to end up with Jake, and there isn't a thing you can do about it." She left then, slamming the door behind her. The draft of air from her slamming the door picked up a piece of paper on the floor and I bent to pick it up.

It was the schedule for the day. I looked at Jake's slot and saw that he was being sent to the bathhouse, the area set up with hot tubs and steam rooms. Beside his name in bold red letters was Arabella's name. I wanted to scream. How cheap could these people get? They'd have her prancing around in a tiny bikini, her boobs and ass on display for the viewers, and Jake would be sitting there, helpless to look away.

I took a deep breath and reminded myself of the hunger in his eyes the night before. That wasn't the gaze of a man willing to throw it all away for someone he didn't care about. I knew he cared about me. Why else would he be so determined to see me after the show ended? But what if she was just too tempting? She was a beautiful woman, after all.

I could feel my toes scrunching in my shoes with

anxiety as the urge to break a glass vase over Carol's head swept over me. This was all her doing and I knew it.

Was it all just a game to Jake, though? Was that part of her little speech true? Maybe he was playing up our attraction for the television.

No, I knew better. Alright, I didn't really know Jake that well, not his birthday, or his job, or what he thought about the state of plastics forming islands in the world's oceans, but I knew he was kind. I knew his eyes lit up in a special way when he saw me and how they didn't when they saw other people. I knew how intimate his touch could be. I also knew he was just as frustrated with this show as I was and ready to go home.

The way Carol and the other producers made his shoulders tense and his jaw turn into a brick when they came near him told me that. The way he sighed unhappily when he was with the other women and always looked for me told me I was special. No, I thought as I settled at the table set for two, Jake wouldn't let a woman like Arabella turn his head. He wasn't like that.

I hoped.

My toes scrunched in my shoes again, but I breathed out deeply. No, we could do this.

I managed to get through the date with Trent, one where he ate noisily, and with some odd chewing technique that reminded me of a squirrel. I fended off his rather timid amorous advances with the feeling he was only doing it for the cameras making me cringe. I also managed to get through the scheduled date with David, mainly because, unlike Trent the octopus, David kept his hands to himself.

David was a true gentleman and he treated me with respect. We both knew he really wanted to be with Kelly, but we gave the producers what they wanted, even if there was zero chemistry between us. We strolled along the edge of the trees, letting them get beautiful shots of a cold but sunny day as we talked about how wonderful Kelly was.

We were wearing portable microphones so we knew they could hear us, but we also knew that none of the audio would be used. The spark just wasn't there for us.

"You know, I've never met anyone that actually made my heart race, Laney. Not like Kelly does anyway. I lose all thought, all of my words, my ability to write beautiful phrases just disappears when she's near. All I can think is, she's so beautiful." He sighed unhappily as we discussed how he could get his knack back.

"Have you tried writing down your thoughts when she isn't around?" I offered, my own woes at the back of my mind for the moment.

"I've tried that, I really have. I just..." He broke off with a sigh. "I want to write her mountains of poetry, but even when I'm not near her all I can think about is her. Obviously, I've monopolized our whole date talking about her. My apologies, Laney." He'd stopped walking and took my hand in his. "I am sorry, you know? You're actually a lovely woman, and you're quite attractive."

He gave me a wink as I felt my cheeks go warm.

"Thanks, David. Kelly is a lucky girl." He was a handsome young man, and I suspected he was also the rich one.

He seemed too shy and introverted to be a teacher, and he seemed to be well educated, so I knew he wasn't a plumber. I couldn't see him knowing the difference between a pipe wrench and a screwdriver.

It was his turn to blush after my compliment, and I knew that gentle, sweet David really was the perfect choice for Kelly. He would be her gentle hero for the rest of her life.

If only I knew my own chance at forever was as real as theirs.

It was ridiculous, being so hopeful after only a couple of weeks, but this place did that to you. Secreted away from everyone you knew, without your normal support systems, and all but cloistered together, bonds were forming that would be hard to break, even after the show ended. I knew Kelly would be a major fixture in the rest of my life, for example, and we'd already exchanged contact information just in case one of us got booted unexpectedly.

David and I started to walk back to the cabin together, both lost in our own thoughts. My gaze kept going to the area where I knew the bathhouse was, though I couldn't really see it, and I wondered what my own future held. Would this all end in heartbreak and humiliation or would it end with happiness and love?

I glanced over at David and smiled. I didn't necessarily want his kind of happiness and love. I liked it a little rough around the edges. A little dirty talk would suit me nicely. I was far from a wilting violet, after all. For a little while, I realized, the romance and the pageantry had turned me into some soppy Jane Austen heroine, but now that was over with. As I walked along the beach, I knew I'd played the game as demanded, but when this was all over, I was totally going to take Jake for my own.

Carol and Arabella could do whatever they liked, they could show the world whatever they wanted to, the winner would be the one that was still standing at the end of it all. I'd come into this with the thought it might be a laugh and it would keep Tony off my back about dating; not anymore. I wanted to understand who Jake was as a man. I'd played life safe for far too long. It was time to take a chance on madness.

CHAPTER EIGHT

JAKE

Arabella's voice droned on and I was well past pretending to even be slightly interested. It was a downright struggle just to keep my eyes open. Sure, the woman was hot; she'd given me her full regimen on how she kept her weight at the perfect balance as she pooled water on her toned flat abdomen. Too many crunches in my opinion. There was nothing soft about her. Even her breasts looked like two hard balls on her chest.

With a sigh, I ran my fingers through my hair as I tried to pretend to concentrate on her tale about how she'd tempted some Italian prince into her bed. Did she really think I'd buy into that? The way she bragged about every aspect of her life turned me off completely.

I didn't want a weak woman who couldn't stand up for herself, or one who waited to be told what to do. I wanted someone who would be my partner, would be by my side for anything and everything. Someone like Laney.

I knew she was out of her depth on this show, and that she was very reserved around others, but I'd seen her when she didn't think anyone was watching. She was observant, quiet, and always aware. When she was talking with Kelly, her face lit up. I saw the woman who attracted me the most; confident, assured, and happy with life. I'd also seen her when she thought she was hiding her anger, when she was trying to bite her tongue around Carol and Arabella. She was a fighter and I knew it.

Just the kind of woman I wanted at my side to face the world I'd found myself in.

I listened to Arabella as she told me about how her family was rich and always had been. How her father had never been able to refuse her. I looked at her, my eyes squinted in a way that should have warned her she was on my last nerve, but she just carried on regardless.

"You know, there's not a man on this planet that has ever been able to say no to me." She swam closer to me, her voice low and husky as she traced a path down my chest.

I'd propped myself against the wall of the pool. I watched her long acrylic fingernail as she wound it down my chest, but grabbed it before she reached the bottom of my ribs.

"Not a single man has ever told you no, huh?" I asked, a dark eyebrow cocked. I gave her a sexy, teasing look, an intense look that made her catch her breath.

"No, not once." She thought she had me now.

"That's... interesting."

Her own eyebrow cocked, a perfect wing over her dark eyes. "Is it?" she asked, caught in my snare now.

"Oh, yes, it is. You see," I said, pulling myself out of the pool, water sluicing down my body, "you're about to find out what no sounds like."

I stood and walked away from her.

She was just too much to take in large doses. I knew I was supposed to spend the entire day with her but I just couldn't.

She'd walked onto the set in a tiny gold bikini, fully on display. I'd barely noticed because I was lost in my memories of Laney panting above me, in the way her stomach muscles had fluttered as she came, the way she cried out my name.

I went into a bathroom and locked the door just for five minutes without her grating voice. I didn't think she realized she sounded as if she'd been smoking five packs of cigarettes a day since she was sixteen and then chewed razor blades as a snack. Fuck, it was annoying.

"Jake, can you come out, please?" I heard Carol's voice through the door, but ignored it.

Why can't these people just give me five minutes of peace? Seriously, my head was going to explode if they kept this up.

"I'll be out in a little while. I just need a minute." I didn't care if she thought I was in here with the worst stomach flu ever. I wasn't leaving this quiet, cool place that wasn't artificially overheated until I was ready.

"We need to keep filming, come on, Jake. Be a big boy for me." Her snide voice came across as demanding, not coaxing.

She wasn't very good at this, no wonder she was working for reality television.

"How about you just fuck off, Carol? I've given you everything you asked for, you have lots of footage of Arabella slithering all over me like a snake. What else do you want?"

Knowing this crazy woman, she probably wanted full on sex.

That wasn't going to happen at all.

"Just give me another half hour. Then we can call it a day." I could all but see her checking her watch through the door. She was likely checking the time to make sure she could keep me away from Laney.

I knew that was what this was all about. Carol had decided I was to choose Arabella, and my fascination with Laney was breaking her balls. She wasn't going to have it.

Normally I would have just walked off by now. I needed to be at home where I could concentrate on my work and on how to convince Laney I was the only one she'd ever need. I'd never believed in old-fashioned love at first sight, but I was starting to. The woman truly did fascinate me.

I knew Gran was at home and probably already bragging to her friends at her bingo nights. Gran wanted this, and she'd never asked me for anything. I could give her the one thing she had asked me for. I knew she'd give Arabella and Carol both a piece of her mind. She wouldn't stand to have her boy talked to like this.

It made me smile to think of her. She'd done so much for me and never complained, not even when she was in the depths of her own grief when her child—my father—died. I settled against the door, my head nestled on the oak panel, as I thought about my grandmother. No, she wouldn't put up with this nonsense from either of those women. She'd likely take a baseball bat to them.

That made me outright laugh.

She would definitely do that, especially if she'd had a nip of gin before she met with the two harridans.

I stood up, swiped at my face once more, took a pull of the hand disinfectant in a dispenser and wished I could bathe in the stuff after suffering Arabella's touchy-feeling escapades, and opened the door.

"Look, I'm done for the day, alright? Unless you want your billionaire to walk off the set, you'll listen to me, got it?" I gave her a look that she could not mistake, and for the first time the woman backed off without another word.

Good.

I went to my room, and despite being in water for far too much of the day, I turned on the en-suite shower and stepped in after I stripped down. I let the hot water wash away that other woman's touch and memory. I'd turned on the music player provided in the room, a selection of my own choosing, and let the music fill my head.

A song by a British band came on, a deep, bluesy sounding guitar introduced a song that asked if the singer wanted to know about the woman that has him obsessed. I could totally get why I loved that song now. I wanted to know more about Laney. I wanted to know if she felt the same.

Most of all, I wanted to know what it would feel like to sink into her wet heat. I groaned, I couldn't help it, and let my hand find the part of me that ached the most. Soap made my light stroke a slick heaven.

What would it feel like when she touched me there? Would it feel even better than I imagined? That led me to wondering what it would be like to watch her swallowing me.

My hand stroked faster, harder, as hot water cascaded down my body, making my nipples tight as I thought about her tongue stroking the tight buds, then down to wrap around my hard cock. More, fuck, more. I pictured her swallowing me, those impish eyes of hers teasing me as my cock disappeared down her throat.

"Fuck!" I spit the word out as I fantasized about the woman with captivating eyes. It was those eyes more than anything that got me.

I knew she'd be sweet, dirty, but oh so fucking sweet.

I'd stroke under her chin as she took my come, as she swallowed all I had to give her, those eyes telling me how much she adored everything I gave her.

I slowed my pace. I wanted this to last. I had a lot of time to kill and a lot of hot water to get through.

I leaned back against the wet wall, trying to slow myself down, but I thought of Laney bent over, her ass high in the air as I bent her over the bed. She'd be whimpering for me to fuck her. I knew she would because I wouldn't put her on her knees until she was begging for it.

"Laney." I whispered her name out loud as I imagined her ass, all that long red hair splayed down her back, pictured how pale her skin would be, and then my cock, sliding between her thighs, straight into her tight walls.

I couldn't stop it, the explosion came, and I was helpless to hold back. Laney was just too much to resist. I'd felt that smooth ass, I'd held it and kneaded it as I made her come on my tongue. I'd just not seen her totally naked.

That would be the first thing I'd rectify when we got out of this hellhole. I would take her somewhere, Paris if she wanted, and strip her down until we were skin to skin.

That's how I wanted her right now. If she said she wanted to do nothing but talk, that's what I would give her. But if she said she wanted more, I would give her more than she'd ever bargained for.

I had to lean against the wall as the final burst jolted me, almost bringing me to my knees. I needed her. Only Laney. Not Arabella, not some other woman, just Laney.

This show couldn't end soon enough.

I finally left the shower, a large chocolate brown towel wrapped around my hips, and stopped short. Arabella was on my bed, on full display in black lingerie that showcased her body well.

I have to admit, for a moment, she made a luscious picture, but then she spoke.

"Don't you think it's time you stopped fighting yourself, Jake? You know you can't turn me away." Her smirk was not sexy, and it was far from becoming.

I leaned against the doorway that led to the bedroom and stared at her.

"Come on, big boy. Show Momma how you do it." She patted the bed, her nails gleaming in the light of the bedside lamp. She'd put a red silk scarf over the light, and it gave the room a romantic glow, but she wasn't the one I wanted to have in my bed.

"First, I'm not your big boy. Second, you're the furthest thing from my mother that could possibly be. Lastly, you can get the fuck out of my room."

Instead of getting up she came around the bed and stood in front of me, her overpowering perfume cloying and stifling.

"Aw, Jakey, come on, baby."

She tried to kiss me, but I pushed her away gently.

"No, Arabella. I know this might be hard for you to grasp, though it is often repeated but no means no. I don't want you, I don't want you in my room. I certainly don't want to fuck you."

Rather than leave, she leaned more deeply into me. "What were you doing in the shower, Jake? Were you touching yourself? Thinking of me?"

She was trying to sound seductive again, but it had no effect on me. In fact, I laughed at her.

"Oh, I was definitely touching myself in there, Arabella." I laughed again, and I hated to be cruel, but directness wasn't working. I leaned over her, my finger pointing her chin up to me. I lowered my head, until our lips almost touched, before I started to speak, our eyes locked together. "I was thinking of Laney, though, not you."

That made her turn on her heel and leave, roughly grabbing her robe as she did so. The door almost shook out of its frame she slammed it so hard, and I let out a loud laugh. Perhaps the loudest laugh I'd let loose since I'd been there.

I pushed the covers down on the bed and looked around the room. A large, antique bed filled it, mosquito netting pinned to four posts on each corner. The comforter was gold, the room decorated with dark wood furniture and dark paneled walls. It was rather like a coffin, at times, but it was only to sleep in.

I pulled out one of the books I'd brought, a horror novel by one of my favorite authors. You'd think with a past like mine that horror would be the last thing I should read. But I'd faced the worst life had to offer at an early age. It had made me hide from life for a long time; my studies, then work had kept me busy.

I'd played the field, yeah, but I'd played it with women that understood I wasn't a second date kind of guy. They'd obliged, as had I, and we'd gone on to live our lives. I'd never really wanted a family. It was something to lose, right?

Laney was changing that, though. I was starting to

think about the long-term, about futures, and maybe, one day, maybe even children. Gran had been right. I needed a woman. I needed Laney.

The Beatles started playing and I smiled. I wasn't going to let Laney down. I settled down into the covers, checked to make sure the door was locked with a glance, and settled down for the night.

It was almost done, thank fuck.

CHAPTER NINE

LANEY

"They've called a meeting!" Kelly came into the bedroom I now had to myself and sat down on my bed. "I think it's another elimination. We have to be ready in twenty minutes."

She didn't look at me as I sat up, my hair wild and my face a sleepy mess. She sat flicking a nail against her thumb nervously. A deep sigh was another clue that she was eaten up with anxiety.

"It'll be okay, Kelly. After what David said yesterday, you have nothing to worry about." I pushed my hair out of my eyes and scrubbed at my face, just in case I'd drooled down one side. I hated that.

"What did he say?" She turned to me, her eyes excited and full of hope.

"I've not had coffee yet so I can't remember exactly, but the man is head over heels for you. Seriously." I pushed the warm comfort of the covers away. I had about fifteen minutes to make myself look presentable. "Now, since you're already functioning, could you find me a cup of coffee while I try to make myself look human again?"

I gave her a pitiful smile and she jumped off the bed before bending down to give me a peck on the top of my head. "I'll be back in five."

After she left I pushed out of the bed and stood up. It was time for my own nerves to take over. A quick sluice in the shower, my hair piled into a knot on the top of my head, and some eyeliner made me look more alive. I hadn't slept well, worrying about what had happened on Jake's date with Arabella had seen to that, and the stress showed on my face. I was as good as I was going to be today.

I slipped into a pair of jeans and a sapphire sweater, black leather boots over my pants my last step before I left my room. I headed to the dining room and hoped I'd be allowed some kind of breakfast before the next bomb was dropped on us. My tummy rumbled as I sat down and smelled the delightful fragrance of ham and the fluffy buttery smell of southern biscuits. Unlike some of the others, I didn't care enough about my figure to deny myself the delight of a ham biscuit. I had a feeling nervous energy would soon do away with the calories anyway.

I was almost finished with the biscuit when Kelly sat down beside me, two cups of coffee in hand. She was about to speak when Skip walked in, drawing our attention.

"Ladies, are you finished eating? You are? Good, because you're all going home now. You will return on Christmas Eve when the conclusion to the show will be broadcast live."

He left without another word as shocked noises filled the air.

I just looked at Kelly, unable to form a thought.

"I have to find David. He has to know how to contact me." She took off, her own red hair a flag behind her.

I decided I needed to do the same thing and went to find a pen and some paper. I quickly scrawled out my name, phone number, and email address on the paper, folded it up, and headed for his room. I tapped at his door and he soon answered, surprise on his face.

"Laney," but I interrupted him.

"There's no time, take this. Call me!" I said and headed back to the dining room, just in case there was more news.

The room was empty when I went in, so I headed back to my own room.

"How do they expect us to be ready in ten minutes? This is crazy!" I heard one girl wailing.

I thought it was too, but went back to my room to

throw my belongings in my suitcase. I could only think about the fact that I would be in my own bed tonight, that I would be able to whack Tony over the head for the mess he got me into, and that I would be away from Carol and Arabella. The only downside was, I'd be nowhere near Jake.

Five minutes later I had everything packed and went to the front of the house to await further instructions. I was the first one there, so I looked around at the house to admire it one last time.

The house had been designed by a man, with male tastes at the forefront. Hardwood floors, wood-paneled walls, few lights, dark heavy furniture, it was all about the man. I liked the place but the only thing that ever drew me in were the windows looking out at the beach. Normally, you'd expect a beach house to be open, light, full of white walls and airy ceilings. This place was almost oppressive. It had always confused me and now that I was leaving, I distracted myself from my panic by mulling it all over.

"Hey! You ready?" Kelly came up beside me, full of her normal bouncy energy and her happy smile.

"Yes, but no. This is making me crazy, you know?" I gave her a look I knew would convey my worry, and she put her hand just above my elbow to comfort me.

"It'll be fine, Laney. I can all but promise you that. Jake is stuck on you, girl. Not on that—" She paused, and

I knew she was looking for a really good insult but not coming up with exactly what to insult Arabella with. "Tramp."

I snorted at her rather fine choice and looked down at my feet to try to stop an outright laugh. "That's pretty accurate, I'd imagine. The cars are here, let's go."

We walked out together, but stopped when Carol stepped out of one of the cars.

"You will be driven to the boats that will take you back to the mainland. You'll then be driven to the airport, and from there to your respective homes. You are to discuss no part of the show with anyone, not even your BFFs, is that clear? Nothing must be leaked about the show or you will be sued and sued royally." Her glare made me roll my eyes. The woman was impossible.

There was no, "it's been great, can't wait to see you again soon," or even a, "I hate you and hope you don't flake out on us," it was just keep quiet or get sued. Typical Carol.

I went into the nearest car with Kelly and we both leaned over the backseat of the black sedan to stare up at the windows we knew to be the bedroom of each of our men.

I saw David smiling and waving down at Kelly and she waved back with a sigh. I didn't see Jake anywhere. I felt my smile crack a little. The car started and the driver put it into gear. That's when Jake appeared in the window, holding up a sign.

'I will find you!'

I smiled fully again and waved. I really hoped he would find me. To see him, alone, without all of the cameras, the snide dealings, and the rest of it would be nice.

I didn't even know his last name, but somehow, Jake had become my world.

Kelly sniffed and I knew she was trying not to cry. I handed her a tissue from my bag as I dabbed at my own eyes.

"Wow, I can't believe I'm about to say this but we have to be brave, Kelly. It's only a few weeks." She took the tissue gratefully and gave me a watery smile in return.

"We can do it. Just make sure you call me or I might go crazy!"

"I will and you know it, girl." I pulled her to my side and hugged her close. "I think I'll need some support too, you know?"

She leaned into me and we absorbed the comfort offered until we arrived at the boat launch.

We had to part ways at the airport as Kelly was given paperwork for a different carrier to mine, and it was just as hard to watch her goes as it was to leave Jake behind. She'd become so integral to my world in such a short time, I didn't know how I'd get through the days to come without her smile.

My flight home wasn't long, just a puddle jump up the coast. Before I knew it, I was standing at my own front door. For a moment, I wondered if it had all been a dream. I didn't even know what day it was.

Tony opened the front door and all but dragged me into the house.

"Girl, it is so good to see you, but why are you home? Were you eliminated? I'll write so many furious emails if they did, they'll think they're being targeted by a hate group. Come on, come in the house, sit down. Let me grab your bag."

He plunked me down on the couch in our familiar home and I looked around as he ran about grabbing my luggage and fixing me a glass of tea.

"Here, drink this. You look shell-shocked. Do you hate me?" He sat across from me on the couch, his leg pulled up in front of him.

"I don't hate you. I do, but not much. I think you're right with the shellshock. We got up this morning only to be told we were leaving. All of us left."

"How many of you are left?" His excitement was obvious from the gleam in his eye and the way he grinned.

"There's five of us now." I sat back on the couch, the

tea cradled on my chest. "I'm on the home stretch at least."

"I knew any man worth being called a man would see you for the gem you are!" He all but clapped in his excitement. "Tell me about it, come on, spill. Tell Tony all the gory details."

I remembered Carol's threat of being sued, but decided to tell Tony anyway. Fuck her! I filled Tony in on everything, from the very beginning to the very last moment when Jake held up that sign.

Tony leaned against the couch, his gorgeous eyes filled with tears. "That is so romantic! You are so lucky, Laney!"

"I think I might be." I was the doing the sighing then, and let my head fall against the couch. "I think I could sleep for a week."

A knock came at the back door and we both jumped.

"Tony? I know you're in there! Was that Laney I saw come in earlier? Buddy, you'd better let me in!"

I chuckled as I stood up to go and let the elderly woman in. She looked spitting mad as she stormed into the house and turned to me.

"Did they send you home because you've been eliminated? That's all I want to know. I guess they've got you under some kind of secrecy mumbo-jumbo, but I have to know if you're still in the running or not."

"Hello to you too, Mrs. Mallory." I leaned down to

give her a kiss on the cheek, which she graciously accepted with a titter and a smile. "And no, I've not been eliminated. They decided to send us home until Christmas Eve when the final choices will be made."

"I see. Good. That's good then, honey. I knew you could do it. You're a catch if I've ever seen one." Mrs. Mallory patted my cheek for a moment and looked up at me with a happy face. "I'll be off then, I know you've only just got home so you'll be tired."

"Why don't you stay and have a glass of tea? I've missed you." The older woman could be a curmudgeon, but she was always kind to me and I adored her, really.

"I'll tell you what, I'll come by later and bring you some real food. You haven't been eating properly from the looks of you." She eyed my waistline with a grimace and shook her head in confirmation. "Yes, you'll be eating meatloaf and homemade rolls before the nights over with, my lovely. I shall return around six."

I couldn't refuse. She would pretend not to hear me if I did, so I gave a noise of understanding and watched her go.

"Tony, you'd best go down to the store and get some gin and tonic. I think our young lady here could use one." Mrs. Mallory made her parting shot just as the screen door closed behind her.

"You know she'll have your ears if you don't," I said to him with a smile.

"I know. I'm so glad it's Monday and I'm off today. I'd have missed all of this otherwise." He went to grab his keys and came back in. "Do you need anything?"

"Ice cream, chocolate cake, and lots of ice if we're having gin and tonics." I gave him a grin. Mrs. Mallory's mixology was legendary at our house. She could make one delicious drink.

"Will do. I'll be back shortly then." He left me in the house and I went back to the couch, it was nice to be in a quiet house without the chatter of voices and the stress of the competition.

The house seemed to settle after that. Cracks and pops sounded like the house knew an occupant had left and it was letting the belt out on its pants. I laughed at the thought and settled deeper into the couch. A nap might be what I needed after the pace of the day so far.

I wouldn't sleep long, just until Tony came home, I promised myself. Just long enough to ease the ache of fatigue and to not have to be alone with my thoughts. Alone with the realization that I wouldn't see Jake again for a long time.

CHAPTER TEN

JAKE

"Jackson Mallory, you get out of that basement right now, son! You can't mope down there forever." Gran's voice penetrated the darkness of my basement cave. I glanced over at my laptop screen, the only light in the darkness, and groaned. I'd missed my nine am alarm by an hour somehow.

"I'll be up in a minute, Gran. I missed my alarm." Even when you work from home alarm clocks are necessary to stay on schedule. Mine had failed me today.

I didn't really care, but Gran liked to have breakfast made and the dishes washed by now so she was going to be off all day. She might be retired but she still worked on a schedule.

"Have you grown a pair yet?" she called down, not leaving the door.

My head swiveled in her direction as my jaw

dropped. Did she? Had she just said what I thought she said?

"Gran?" I called, getting out of the bed and automatically reaching for my hair. Damn, that was a hard habit to break. Gran was happy about it though, and she'd finally put her scissors away when I came home four days ago.

"Have you told that show to shove it yet and contacted Laney?" I heard a low cackle of glee and knew she'd enjoyed shocking me.

"You know I can't, Gran. I can't jeopardize my business over this stupid show. At least, that's what my lawyer said. They've got some very tiny print in a very odd place, that screws, uh, messes me over completely if I don't at least finish the show." I walked up the stairs and into the bathroom to brush my teeth.

"Well, I can't say I'm sorry. You did meet this Laney girl, after all." To a woman Gran's age, anybody under fifty was a boy or a girl. I started to brush my teeth as she went on. "You are still taken with her, right?"

I gave a nod as I spit out toothpaste bubbles and rinsed my mouth. "Completely, Gran, that's the only reason I haven't throttled you yet."

I washed my face and then went with her to the kitchen. "Sorry I wasn't up earlier. My alarm just didn't want to go off today."

"It's alright, boy. I know you didn't do it on purpose."

Her fingers brushed over my hair lovingly as she walked by me. So many times I'd checked to make sure she hadn't cut off my hair in a sneak attack and now I didn't have to worry about that. She still made me nervous with those scissors, though.

"I can't contact her at all. It's crazy. I don't know how they'd find out if I did, but still. I hate this, but you're right, at least I met Laney." I watched her as she started making biscuits, a measuring cup nowhere in sight, and wondered how many more times she'd get to make me breakfast.

A rather morbid thought, but a sensible one. Gran wasn't going to live forever, that was part of the reason I was here now, to help her out as she aged. I'd needed a place to hide from a money-hungry public and she'd needed me, so here I was. She wouldn't admit it now, but she needed far more help than she'd ever ask for.

"I'll get that wood chopped and stacked up for you."

Gran still used a wood-stove to heat the house in the winter and hated electric heat. A little exercise would do me a world of good and keep my mind off my problems.

"You're such a good boy, Jake." Her fingers were covered in biscuit dough, but there were now eight perfectly shaped biscuits in the pan.

She put the biscuits in the oven and washed her hands. I poured us both a cup of coffee and set it on the table as she sat down, the smell of frying sausage filling the air with sage and rosemary.

"How many eggs do you want this morning?" she asked, inspecting her nails for stray flour.

"Three. That pile of wood is pretty massive." I grinned as she squinted at me, her cantankerous persona back in place.

"Gonna eat me out of house and home, boy!"

We both knew I paid the bills for her, but I let her have her fun.

"You always said food is fuel, Gran. If you want me to cut up that wood for fuel, I need some fuel."

She glared at me before she finned back.

"I suppose you do." She went through the motions from memory, turning the sausage, frying eggs, checking the biscuits, before she put the sausage on a plate and down into the oven she turned off. The rest would stay warm while she prepared the gravy.

We had a beautiful breakfast, broken only by the sounds of delight I made as I sank my teeth into gravy covered biscuits. I'd have to cook this for Laney one morning. Gran had taught me long ago how to cook for myself, but she'd never let me cook for her, not unless she was sick.

"Have you got bingo today?" I asked as she picked up her now empty plate and headed to the sink.

"Mary Beth is bringing the gin today," she answered

in a distracted tone, her gaze on the house next door. "Why don't you get started on that wood, Jake, and I'll get these dishes cleaned up."

"I wish you'd let me buy you a dishwasher..." I started, but she cut in, the argument an old one.

"I don't need none of that foolery, Jake. I have two hands, soap, and one of those sponge thingies. I can manage. Besides, it keeps my fingers nimble." She cackled as though she'd made a dirty joke and I tried not to think about it.

Putting a flannel shirt over my long-sleeved T-shirt, I went outside and stuffed my feet into work boots before I grabbed the ax. A little bit of hard work would clear my head for the day. I was ignoring work I should be doing with my own business, but it was under control. I had built up a rhythm and had destroyed most of the pile when a sound stopped me mid-swing.

I turned to see the neighbor coming out of the house and going to her car. She looked strangely familiar, and I walked up the large oak on Gran's side of the yard to get a better look at her. I stood there, stunned, as I watched Laney back the car up and drive away.

My first instinct was to run after her, to scream out her name until she stopped, but common sense held me back. My lawyer had been very specific about exactly what I'd lose, and I couldn't jeopardize the years Gran had left by doing that. Even for love.

I watched her drive away and felt anger burn through me. I shouldn't have to make these decisions, I shouldn't have to choose between love and my Gran's wellbeing. I had more money than some whole countries. I could build that all up again, right?

This was Laney, after all. Not a woman like Arabella, or the ones from the online dating sites offering to be my sex slave for a chance at plastic happiness. I looked back at the house and saw Gran in the window. She was beckoning me to come into the house.

"Son, sit down."

"How did the show not figure it out, Gran?" I asked as I sat down in a rocking chair that was probably new twenty years before I was born.

"That the addresses were so similar? I guess none of them took the time to notice." She was in her own rocker, covered in that awful shade of green velvet that was popular back in the seventies.

I was too stunned to think any further than that. Laney was only next door. Just next door. I could talk to her when I wanted to, I could see her anytime I wanted to. I could touch her and smell her. All I had to give up was the ability to take care of Gran in the manner she deserved.

She didn't have to sneak gin into her bingo games, she did it because she loved the naughtiness of it. She could set up her own bingo hall if she wanted, one with a bar, but she preferred doing it the way she did because it was fun. I'd offered her a brand new home, a brand new car, and everything she could possibly want and all she'd asked for was my time to nail down her carpet again.

One day she might need far more care than I could provide for her. If she was lucky, she'd go peacefully in her sleep in twenty years. That wasn't guaranteed though, and I liked knowing if she ever changed her mind I could buy my Gran a mansion, a Ferrari, and a strip club full of bingo callers if she so desired. She thought I didn't know about those, but I'd heard her talking with her lady friends.

I felt my lips quirk at that and looked at her. "You knew she was just there then?"

"Oh, Tony, her roommate, and I have had this planned for a while now. He set her up to go on the show, and I set you up. We've been trying to get you two together for a long time and neither of you would play along. We thought if you were on the show, then you'd have to spend time together. We were right, weren't we?" She gave me a gimlet-eyed look and I wanted to kiss her sweet, wrinkled cheeks.

"You were, Gran. The question is, what do we do now?"

"Nothing, if that's what you want to do, we hide you away here, you get to keep all those piles of money, and you finish the show." She sighed and looked away for a minute. I knew she thought that was a bad idea. "Or you stop worrying about me and do something for yourself. You've been taking care of me since you were young, always there to help, being such a good kid, and making sure you did everything you were supposed to. You never took the time to have real fun, or fall in love. It's time you did, Jackson."

She only used my real name when she was being serious, or trying to get my attention. It worked as always.

"But, what if you get sick, Gran, and need nurses? An operation? You can't afford that." I felt helpless just thinking about it.

"Jake, you know as well as I do that you can't run from love, and you can't run from death. If it comes for me, it will. I have some money left from your grandfather's, and a little of my own saved up. I'll be fine. I want you to have what your parents missed out on, son. A long life with kids and a happy future. Don't throw that away over an old woman at the end of her own life."

Her words stung a bit, the reminder that my parents had died a horrible death was never easy to take, but Gran's words couldn't be truer. For the first time in my life, I knew I was in love. Could I do that to Gran though? She'd been through a lot in her life, she'd lost her husband when she was in her early forties, their May-December romance leaving her a widow at a young age, and then she'd lost my father and her daughter-in-law in a fire that nearly took me with it. I owed her my loyalty and devotion, didn't I?

"There's always the chance they won't figure it out, Jake. If you're willing to take that chance."

I nodded in agreement, lost in thought. I couldn't do that to Gran, no matter what she said about it. But maybe, maybe we could keep it quiet.

"How about we go buy a Christmas tree, Gran? I think I'd like to have one this year." We didn't always decorate for the holiday, the memory of those we'd lost, both my parents and my grandfather, was too overwhelming some years, but this year we both had hope for a brighter future, and I really wanted to believe in the magic of the Christmas season, something I'd given up a long time ago.

Laney was bringing all of that back for me and I could see that Gran felt much the same way about it.

"You mean the whole shebang, don't you? We're going to buy more than a Christmas tree. You know most of my decorations are older than you." She looked like she was twelve years old again and staring into the old storefront window from the past she loved to talk about. I could all but see her nose squished up against a window as she looked in.

I couldn't stop the smile on my face as she stood up and went to her room to put on her 'going out' clothes.

I didn't know exactly what I'd decide to do, but for now, I could bring the spirit of Christmas into the house and pray like mad that it worked. Something had to, I couldn't live so close to Laney without going over there and kissing her. Besides, I think Gran and I both needed it this year. We'd had one too many dark, lonely Christmases in the past. One way or another, I was going to give Gran the best one she'd ever had. If the show ended the way I wanted it to, I'd be spending it with both Gran and Laney. That was something to believe in.

CHAPTER ELEVEN

LANEY

I spent a few days moping around the house, glaring at Tony for no good reason, and just plain being miserable before I got up the gumption to call my boss and ask if I could come into work. We'd planned on me being gone until January second, but I couldn't sit at home doing nothing.

I did things like check my bank account when I was bored and miserable. Only, instead of staring at an empty account, I saw my mother had been busy sneaking money into it again. At this rate, I'd have enough for an entire year's income at minimum wage in about a week.

No, sitting around doing nothing just wasn't my style. I could probably study for school, if I could concentrate that would have been the smart thing to do, but I couldn't get Jake out of my head. Why hadn't he emailed me yet? Was he still on the island? Were they keeping him there until the show ended?

I went through a thousand scenarios, including one where Carol found my little note and tore it into pieces, but I just didn't know anything for certain. I did a lot of running, a lot of housework, and a lot of binge-watching television shows I wouldn't normally bother with and I still couldn't keep that final scenario out of my mind.

What if he'd spent the night with Arabella and he was done with me?

As I drove into work alone with sad music on, I felt the tears start once more. Tony had tried to cheer me up by reminding me we needed to decorate the house, but I just couldn't bring myself to care. Mom and Dad wanted me to go home, of course, but I had to go back to the show the day before Christmas, so that wasn't going to happen. No, I'd turned into a miserable, irritating cow and the best thing I could do was stack books.

So that's what I did. I went into work and cleaned shelves, dusted offices and rooms. I went through entire sections to make sure the books were all in the correct order, and I smiled happily at customers who couldn't understand why I wanted to set fire to their awful but comedic Christmas sweaters. I just wanted Jake and I couldn't even hear his voice, much less be near him.

I was finally sent home by my boss, because I was driving the other workers crazy with my cleaning craze. Sure, it needed to be done, but they could all tell I was stressed and it was making all of them nervous. I went home and sat on the back porch, waiting for inspiration to hit.

I had worked out a good impression of a statue by the time I saw Jane Mallory walking up the porch steps.

"What are you doing, ladybug?" she asked as she sat down. "It's too cold to be sitting out here."

I gave her a dazed look, confused about where she'd come from. One minute I was alone and the next, she was there. And why had she called me ladybug? Then I remembered it was Jane, and you could never be certain what the impish little elderly woman might come out with.

"I went on that show and met the most..." I paused, trying to think of the right word. There wasn't one single word to describe Jake. "The most gorgeous, sexy, beautiful, intelligent, *good* man I've ever met in my life, Mrs. Mallory. He was just, well, perfect really."

"What's the problem then?" She stood with me and we went inside, out of the cold. I automatically started to make us both some mocha coffee. It was a winter tradition at our house. She'd come over, we'd have mocha coffee, and we'd talk.

"I haven't heard from him since I came home," I said

as I poured hot water into the French press, staring off into space, that dreaded scenario threatening my peace of mind once more.

"Maybe he's not allowed to," she prompted, giving me a look I didn't understand.

"Maybe, it's one thing I considered. There's another woman there, Arabella, that they kept pushing at him. I know he's not interested, but she is beautiful. Maybe he likes her better."

"Have you ever been in love before, Laney?"

I looked at her, wondering at the question. "I don't think so, not the kind in movies or novels, anyway."

"You've never felt your stomach plummet when you see your boyfriend, or your heart flutter as they walk near?" She had a gleam in her eye, one that confused me.

"Only with Jake. Only him."

She gave me a look of approval before she carried on. "Do you think he's the rich one?" she asked carefully, as though it were a trick question.

"No, I think the rich one is that butthead named Trent. He's so obnoxious. Only the rich could have that attitude. David has to be the teacher, though I'm not certain he could actually stand in front of an audience that long without dying of embarrassment. He's sweet, really. I think Jake's the plumber."

"Not a bad profession. An honest one anyway." She watched me carefully as she spoke.

"I'm sure they see some sights." I finally poured the water into the French Press and slid the plunger down.

"It doesn't bother you, that he might be a plumber?"

"Not at all. As you say, it's an honest profession. He'll always have work, especially down here."

"Why haven't you ever been in love before, then, Laney?" She looked curious again and I thought about it hard.

"I guess because I've always been so convinced I needed to study. My mom's a cardiologist, one of the top in her field. She never pushed me, but you know, just knowing how successful she is, that's a lot to compete with. I'm also independent. I don't like counting on others." I finished making the mocha coffee and put a glass mug in front of Mrs. Mallory that was topped with whipped cream.

"I understand that, Laney. You need to experience love though, and it sounds like this Jake is the one for you. If he can bring out that kind of emotion in a girl so determined to make her own way in the world, then he must be special." She sipped at her coffee with a contented sigh.

"He's extraordinary, really." I went to the table where she sat and got in my own chair. Our kitchens were very similar, the difference being that we had a woven-grass topped table for two and she had a wooden one that could feed an army.

"Then it's time to put away childish things and carry on with your life," she said sagely.

"My law degree isn't childish!" I shot back, slightly confused; she was normally so encouraging about my plans.

"Oh, I don't mean that, child, I mean this need to live up to *your* expectations, this need to be as good as your mother. You are both intelligent women, obviously, but you aren't your mother, Laney. You're you and I happen to think you're fantastic!"

Truly high praise from Mrs. Mallory!

"Ah. Good."

"I think your young man will understand he needs to let you finish school and have your own success, if he's as good as you say he is." That odd look again, like she knew something I didn't. "If he doesn't then he isn't worth your time anyway."

"I'm sure you're right. He doesn't seem like the kind of guy that would want me to give up my dreams, anyway. You're right about the whole thing with Mom too. She's tried to tell me the same thing thousands of times, how I needed to take the time to be young, fall in love, all of that." I waved my hand around and Mrs. Mallory spoke again.

"She's right, ladybug. You have to live your whole life, not just portions of it. I fell in love with a man older than me by about twenty years and I lost him early in my life. A lot of people said I was wasting my time with him, but you know, I've never remarried because nobody could ever love me like he did." Her eyes took on a faraway look before she continued. "I wouldn't trade that time with him for the world. I hope you can find that same kind of love, Laney."

She took my hand and I looked at her, stunned at just how much she meant that. The normally feisty, outrageous woman had suddenly become sentimental and loving, and I didn't know how to take it. I let her take my hand and for a moment, I felt peace for the first time since I'd come home.

"Thanks for coming by, Mrs. Mallory. You've really been helpful." I really meant it. "Want more coffee?"

"No, I'd better get home. My grandson is back and I need to make dinner for him."

"You shouldn't be making dinner for him!" I was a bit outraged at the freeloader I assumed he must be to let his seventy-year-old grandmother prepare dinner for him.

"Oh, it's no trouble. He just bought me a new stove, you know? My old one finally broke beyond repair. I think, over the years, it's been repaired so many times it's probably actually been three or four different stoves. I'm just going to pop a pizza in the oven and we're going to watch movies." She stood up and I stood with her.

"Don't lose faith, Laney. I just know he's waiting on you too."

She left and I cleaned up our cups before I prepared dinner for Tony and me.

Tony came home an hour later with a huge Christmas tree, bags full of decorations, and a grin that would not stop.

"We are getting you out of this funk, Laney. I can't stand it anymore. Come on, leave dinner for now. We're giving you back the spirit of Christmas."

"You've transported Jake onto the front porch?" I asked sarcastically.

"No, I've done something better." He popped a Christmas music into a CD player and played it as he found the right spot for the Christmas tree.

Then he started to pull things out of bags. Balls, tinsel, icicles, angels, snowmen, and every kind of decoration I could think of. He'd bought figurines, an entire Christmas village, elves, more snowmen, reindeer, Santas, and even decorations to put in all of our windows.

"Did you rob an entire charity shop?" I asked as I looked at it all. He really was planning on building some kind of wonderland.

"Basically, that one over on Fifth Street. The one that helps the elderly pay their electric bills." He was still pulling stuff out of bags.

"Is that bubble lights?" I loved those when I was a kid, my mom had inherited her mother's. Oil in a glass 'candle' heated up and made bubbles in the lit-up glass. "I love those!"

"There's like four strands of them. Here, start putting this stuff on the tree." Tony handed me a box of glittery red balls and I really did start to feel my Christmas cheer returning.

Before I knew it, I was dancing with Tony around a very well decorated living room, Christmas lights the only illumination, but there were so many lights, on the tree and in the window, that we really didn't need anything else on. I felt like a little girl again, staring at it all in wonder as Tony twirled me around the living room.

I laughed, really laughed, as my best friend did his best to cheer me up. He did a good job.

We finally settled down on the couch, ate the lemon pepper chicken that had been perfect two hours before but was now dried out, and watched old Christmas movies. I was curled up at his side, his hands twirling my hair into twists, when the last movie finished.

"Do you think he's really going to pick me, Tony?" I finally asked, looking at the start screen of the last movie.

"Of course, and I'm not just saying that because you're my best friend. I'm saying it because you're smart, beautiful, and interesting. From what you've said about this Jake, it sounds to me like he appreciates that."

"It's just so hard not knowing what's going on. I'd almost say I hate you for this, but I just can't, because I think I'm really in love with this guy. God, it's just so gross!" I sat up on the couch and pulled one of our over-stuffed red couch pillows into my lap to slouch over it.

"Love usually is gross, sweetie. And messy. And oh my, so dirty." He got up off the couch and went into the kitchen then came back with another bottle of white wine. "I need this now."

He fanned his face as he sat down and I couldn't help but laugh. "Give me that bottle, you're never going to get it open like that."

I worked the cork free and poured the wine into our glasses.

"What am I going to do?" I asked as I took a sip.

"You're going to be the big girl I know you are and you're going to get through this. It's only a few more weeks." He pulled me into a slouchy hug and kissed the top of my head. "Come on, let's binge watch that show about the women in prison, I've heard it's incredible."

I knew he was right, I needed to stop worrying and get on with life. I'd had a lot of good advice lately. It was time I started to listen to it.

* * *

THE NEXT DAY I was helping Tony put reindeer, Santa, and his sleigh on the roof when the world tilted on its side. My foot slipped and for a moment I felt the world slipping away. Tony heard my squeak of fear and grabbed at me. I held onto his hand for dear life before I realized I wasn't sliding anymore.

"You're okay, honey, you have a safety harness on anyway, you aren't going to fall... far." He chuckled as I stood back up.

"That was close." I settled on the apex of the roof and looked down over at Mrs. Mallory's house.

That's when my heart stood still. There was a man next door, piling wood into his arms.

"Is that the grandson?" I whispered over to Tony.

He went still before he sat down beside me.

"Yeah, I think it is."

He had a knit cap on his head, and he didn't look up at us so I didn't get a good look at him at first.

"Have you seen the front yet?" The guy was wearing one of those stretchy thermal tops, in a dark olive green that showed off his muscled chest to perfection. When he stood up, his arms full of wood, something about the set of his shoulders seemed familiar.

"It's just because he's Mrs. Mallory's grandson, right?"

"What's that?" Tony asked, looking at me.

"He seems so...oh my God!" I stood abruptly, almost sliding off the roof again but the harness caught me. "That's Jake. It's Jake!"

CHAPTER TWELVE

JAKE

I heard Laney call out my name and lost my footing. The wood went one way and I went the other as I stared up at the sky. Her voice had come from up there somewhere.

The landing knocked the breath out of me and I could only try to inhale as I searched the sky for the woman of my dreams. I finally spotted her on the roof, her face terrified as she stared down at me.

"Jake? What are you doing down there?" she called down to me with confusion.

"What are you doing up there?" I tried to wheeze out. "You look beautiful by the way!"

She pushed a pair of glasses up her nose, straightened her skewed ponytail, and started towards the ladder.

I clambered up from the ground as she climbed

down the ladder. We stopped just as we came within five feet of each other. In that instant, all my thoughts disappeared, all the doubts, the worries, and fears because Laney was there. Her blue eyes were as beautiful as I remembered, her lips were just as tempting, and I wanted nothing more than to pick her up and carry her to my bed. Now that she was here though, all I wanted to do was stare at her like a creeper.

CHAPTER THIRTEEN

"What are you…? How did you know…? What are you doing at Mrs. Mallory's house, Jake?" I stammered the words out, befuddled but a thought forming. "Are you Mrs. Mallory's grandson?"

He looked like he wanted nothing more than to drag me into his arms. I wouldn't mind it if he did. An explanation of some kind would be nice, though.

"I am, yes." He didn't elaborate.

I made a rolling motion with my hand. "Go on. Wait, I thought her grandson's name was Jackson?"

"It is, but I go by Jake. Look, I can't tell you a whole lot, the show will sue the pants off of me, literally from what my lawyer says." He stopped and scratched at the knit cap on his head.

"Jake? How long have you been over here? Just across from me? How long?" The question had started to burn in my head, anger fanning the flames. Had he been there this whole time and hadn't bothered to tell me?

Was I some kind of fool? Was I just some kind of game the show producers had him playing along with? I knew I didn't know a lot about him, but that didn't seem possible.

"It was a choice between a few stolen moments with you, Laney, and being able to provide for my grandmother. If the show sues me, anything I have or will make could be forfeited. I can't leave Gran in that state. I just can't." He turned away, his shoulders slumped in a way I hated.

I felt a pain start around my heart, an aching squeeze that nearly took my breath away as I watched him. I couldn't let him go on like that.

"I understand that, Jake. That's all I needed, just an explanation." I put my hand out for his and waited.

"Do you know how beautiful you are, Laney? I mean, you're pretty hot when you have your hair done up and makeup on, but like this? I just, I can't believe you're real, woman!"

He took me in his arms at last, and I sank into him, peace sweeping over me as I scoffed at his comments. "I'm dressed in old jeans, a flannel shirt, and I look a mess, Jake."

"You look real, Laney, you look like a woman that needs to be taken to bed..." His words were low, quiet, and seductive. "You look like I need to fuck you until your cheeks are flushed and you can't breathe, only scream my name."

Heat flashed through me. No man had ever been so bold, so graphic, so downright sexy as to say something like that to me, and my knees literally went weak when Jake did it.

"Can we, uh, can we go somewhere Jake? Somewhere *private?*" I looked around and saw Tony coming down off the roof, and Mrs. Mallory was in the window of her kitchen, grinning at us as she waved happily.

She'd known! All that time I'd talked to her about Jake, she'd known it was her grandson. I'd throttle her later, I decided as Jake stepped away.

"Yeah, let me just get my keys. We can go to my new house."

"New?" I asked, a bit lost. "Didn't you just move in here with your grandmother?"

"Yes, but I asked my personal assistant to find me somewhere private, secluded, and out of the spotlight for... well, for times when I needed privacy. It's a little bit of a drive, but it's what I wanted." He looked like he'd bit off something more he wanted to say, but I didn't push. "I'll be right back."

I'd thought about this moment for days now, and somehow, the fates had seen to it to make it all real. I saw him go in and hug his grandmother before he left again, coming back with a coat and a jacket in his hands.

"Look," he said as he grabbed my hand and pulled me towards the brand new Jeep I'd seen in the driveway. "There are things I want to tell you, things I want to say, but I just can't right now. Even doing this may cost me dearly, but..."

"We don't have to do this," I said as he paused to get into the driver's seat. "I can wait or whatever you want to do."

"I haven't been able to get you out of my head, Laney. I dream about you, I think about you during the day, I wonder what you're doing at night. And damn, Laney, I've wanted you since I first saw you. I want this, but it's dangerous."

I understood then, even if he hadn't told me outright. I understood that Jake must be the rich one. Or a very successful plumber. Or a teacher with a very successful book under his belt. He had a PA, a new house, a new car, and all of this other stuff. Yeah, he had a lot to lose. Billions, maybe.

"Uh, Jake. Are you sure about this?" I didn't want to be the reason he lost everything he'd worked for; he'd earned whatever he had. I looked at him and saw only the man I was certain I was in love with. A handsome man with soulful eyes and good taste in clothing. And sexy hair and a beautiful mouth I wanted to kiss until I couldn't kiss him anymore.

"Gran told me it was about time I grew a pair. I have to try to stay within the bounds of that stupid contract, but yeah, I'm certain. Gran says you're more than worth it, after all." He started the car and we pulled away.

Jake was a very good driver, and we were soon in a forest of pine trees as he pulled onto a dirt road. He'd been silent as he made the forty-five minute drive, but he'd look over at me and smile at times, and touch me softly, as if he couldn't believe I was real. I found myself doing the same, and as he pulled into the driveway in front of a single-story cabin clad in cypress I knew this was where I always wanted to be. Wherever Jake was.

"I came over the other day so there's food and other supplies here now. Let me get a fire going and we'll have something to eat, shall we?" He waited for me to get out of the car and then we were walking up the steps to a wide front porch that ran along the front.

"It's a beautiful place, Jake." I didn't ask any questions such as 'did you buy it or are you renting it' because I knew that would give the game away even more.

Jake pushed the door open and I saw a hallway split the cabin in half. On one side there were two doors and in the very back, the kitchen. On the right side, there was only one door and what I could see was a very open room.

"Thanks." Again, he bit off his words, and I knew this was difficult for him.

"I'll get the fire started if you want to see what's in the freezer that you might like. The bathroom is the second door to the left, the kitchen is straight back." He went through to the another room and I could hear him in there working.

I went into the kitchen, a room that ran along the entire back end of the cabin, a dining area to the right was lit by sunlight from a very large window that took up most of the wall. Stainless steel gleamed in the kitchen area, from the fridge to the stove, and even the countertops. It was all very chic and professional looking. I went to the fridge and found the freezer section.

Steak, chops, and frozen meals from a rather posh looking company. I saw one that proclaimed it was the best chicken alfredo in the world and checked the instructions. I put the oven on and waited. Jake soon came through and took a bottle of water out of the fridge.

"I can cook for you if you prefer, Laney. Those frozen dinners aren't bad, but I don't mind cooking, I swear." He looked down at the box doubtfully.

"No, this is fine. Besides, I'm not really hungry right now. Just, a little nervous I guess."

"There's no Carol here, no one to interrupt us, I didn't even bring my phone." He moved towards me and

I looked up at him happily. "It's just you and me and whatever we want to do, Laney."

"Don't you want to watch the show?" I asked impishly, my eyes laughing up at him.

"You aren't really watching it, are you? I can't even stand to hear the introduction music. It's all just so awful. If that's what you want to do, I guess we can watch it. There are so many better things to do though."

I put my arms around his waist and pulled him to me. "You're right, Jake, and all I want to do is kiss you."

I pushed up on my tiptoes and pressed my lips to his. I felt a thrill rush straight down my abdomen as I felt the warm softness of his lips against mine. I could feel his body, so close, and smell his scent.

"I'm not hungry at all, actually." I pulled away and looked at him, wanting him to push me against the counter and kiss me all over again.

He growled low in his throat as his green eyes met my gaze, and he leaned over me. "I've waited so long for you, Laney. So fucking long."

He put a hand either side of me as I leaned against the kitchen counter, and then he was kissing me, but not touching me. Damn, it was amazing!

I couldn't keep up the no contact, not when his tongue was playing over mine, and put my right hand up to his cheek, feeling the slight scrub of a five o'clock shadow. His hands tensed at my hips as I touched him, and he pulled me up to sit on the counter. Our bodies molded together as the kiss continued and heat built within me. I could feel him hard and ready, pressed into my center where I ached for him the most.

I felt his right hand slide down the back of my jeans, to cup my ass and tilt my hips forward, to tease me as his fingers dug into my flesh.

"Jake..." I broke away from the kiss at last, my chest heaving as I tried to breathe.

"Almost," he said, looking down at me intently. "Your cheeks are definitely flushed, but panting my name isn't the same as screaming it. It's damned sexy though."

His fingers tensed on my ass once more and I wrapped my legs around his waist and bent back toward the wall. I wanted to ride the hard ridge until I lost all sense of time and place. I wanted more. I didn't want just a dirty romp in the kitchen.

Hot lips trailed down the length of my throat as his fingers found the buttons of my top.

"I love buttons," he murmured as his lips reached my collarbone. His fingers trailed over the buttons but didn't unfasten them yet. "It's like opening a present when there are buttons."

His lips skimmed beneath the collar of my shirt, over skin that already felt too hot. I held my breath, waiting on his next move.

His finger flicked at the top button and it popped loose, revealing bare skin. "You taste so good, Laney."

I pressed my hips into his, I wanted more. I wanted those buttons to fly away, I wanted the lace of my bra to evaporate, and our clothes to just go away. I wanted to feel his bare skin next to mine.

"Jake, please." I breathed the word against the top of his head as his fingers popped buttons free of their closures, and then he was all that surrounded me as he touched my bare skin with sure fingers. I ran my fingers through his hair, pressing his face into my cleavage.

He inhaled deeply before he moved, to the left, to push silk away from flesh. My fingers clenched in his hair as hot, wet lips surrounded the tight flesh of my nipple.

"Fuck, that feels so good."

He only moaned in response to my words. He couldn't move because my hands were pressing his head into my breast. Instead, he sucked harder at my nipple until my hips were moving against his body, until I was making the most delicious noises I've ever heard myself make.

Then his fingers found the other nipple and I felt pleasure tear through me. I was lost in some swirling maelstrom of suction, of teasing fingers on my other nipple, and the pure presence of Jake. The last time we'd been this intimate we were hindered by the threat of being caught, and now we didn't have that threat, I could concentrate solely on Jake and what he was doing to me. I gasped his name again, just as I felt every part of me start to ripple in pleasure.

All he'd done was touch my breasts and I was already coming hard against him.

"Oh, that is beautiful." Jake let my nipple pop from his mouth long enough to murmur his satisfaction, and then he was pressing his hard cock into me while his lips took the sensitive morsel into the heated cavern of his mouth once more.

I panted as wave after wave tore through my body, uncontrollable, but so damned good!

Jake flexed his hips into mine until I collapsed against the counter, totally wrung out. He let my nipple go and leaned over me with a satisfied grin.

"Are you smirking at me?" I asked, dazed.

"I might be. I've never made a woman come just from sucking her nipples before." He pressed into my overheated center as he spoke and closed his eyes in delight as he felt the pressure.

"I've never done that before. Come from that, I mean. You're very good at it." I felt my cheeks burn as I said the words.

"I aim to please, ma'am." He tilted an imaginary cowboy hat and looked down at me. His eyes went wide as he looked at me on his kitchen counter, totally debauched with my bra pushed aside and my breasts out, while grinning in satisfaction.

"That's not the end of it, right?" I waited for his answer, heat burning between us where our bodies came together.

"Maybe." He gave me a wink as he stepped away.

"Jake, no!" I cried and sat up as I tried to stop him.

"Laney, you don't really think I could say no to you when you're so very temptingly laid out on my counter, do you? Come on, I know a much better place for this."

I jumped down from the counter and followed him into the other room after I took his hand. The fire was the only light in the room, the curtains at the window blocking out the sun completely, and I saw a large bed in the middle of the room.

King sized and covered in white sheets, the headboard and foot of the bed were made from oak wood. The mattress was a plush memory foam that I could feel myself sinking into as I sat down. I stared up at Jake and waited for whatever came next. I wanted it, whatever it was he wanted to offer me.

He smiled, a sexy smile of pleasure as he came to lean over me again. I fell back against the bed when he moved forward, wanting nothing more than to feel Jake over me. He followed me, but only long enough to kiss me. He began to slide down my body, the panels of my shirt opened as his fingers released the rest of the buttons.

I pushed at his shirt with greedy hands, I wanted to feel his skin. I found the buttons of his shirt and sped through them before I pushed his shirt away from his shoulders. Strong and muscled, Jake was perfection in firelight. At last, my fingers touched his smooth skin and the touch was a pleasure I couldn't deny. I moaned as my fingers trailed down his shoulders and arms, then around to his back.

Jake had other ideas, though, and he was soon sinking down my body, pushing my jeans and panties away as he did so. He sank to his knees on the floor, his bare chest gleamed in the firelight. His hands parted my thighs slowly, and his eyes blazed as he saw me fully for the first time.

His fingers trailed down my folds, barely splitting me open. I could feel how slick I was already and let my head fall back, but kept my eyes open to watch him. He studied my body, from the tips of my full breasts, over the softness of my belly, and down to where his fingers were sliding me open.

My hips thrust up into the air of their own accord as Jake's middle finger slipped into me, the intimate touch made more erotic for watching him.

"I want to taste you, to suck your wet pussy until I

drown in you, Laney. I don't think I can wait that long to fuck you. I'm going to try, though."

Before I could protest and tell him how much I wanted to feel him inside me, he stole my thoughts by running his tongue up my slit. I lost the ability to breathe when he sucked at my clit, his hand tilting my ass so he had a better angle.

With determined swipes of his tongue and his thumb probing at my opening, Jake drove me to a pleasure I'd only experienced the last time his tongue was on me. I thought it was just the heightened thrill of being caught that had made me come so fast and so hard then, but it was the same now. Almost every place Jake touched me turned into an erogenous zone capable of getting me off.

Even now I could feel the threatening pressure of an impending orgasm as my hips moved in time with the flick of his tongue. I groaned with each sucking pull of his lips, and then, I was gone. I spiraled into a world where only Jake and the pleasure he gave me existed.

His tongue lashed at me, drove me higher, over the edge again and again, until I was grasping at his head to make him stop. Only he didn't stop. He sucked harder at the center of my pleasure, his hands gripped my hips to hold me in place. I felt him growl against me as he sucked up the juices of my pleasure, and then I was gone again.

I felt my throat go raw as I gasped and cried out things I forgot as soon as I said them. All I wanted was to never stop feeling this way.

My thighs clasped around his head as one final bolt of pleasure shot through me, and I fell back exhausted onto the bed. I couldn't even speak the words I wanted to say. Thank you, don't stop, more, I love you. All I could do was try to remember how to breathe as he came up beside me, his clothes gone and his body on full display.

I saw how glorious a naked Jake was a few moments later when I could finally open my eyes. First one, then the other cracked open as he stroked my hair and waited for me to come back to life.

"Shall we continue or do you want to sleep?" he asked with a wicked smile.

"Do you really think I could say no to you after that, Jake? No way." I pushed up to kiss him, my eyes and hands hungry for him.

He fell back this time and I straddled him, his cock hard between us. I moaned again, my body already primed for him, but I only slid over him slickly, a twist of my hips that made him gasp as his eyes went round.

"Laney, don't you think we should..."

I put my finger over his lips as he held up a condom. "Probably, but not just yet, Jake. I want to explore you now."

I let my hands wander over him, over his hard pecs, down his flat abdomen, around to cup and squeeze his hard ass.

Jake was proud of his body, and he should be, the man was one line of muscle after another. His arms, his torso, and fuck, those thighs. Even his calves were full, hard muscles, not the thin twigs of some men. Jake's body was made for power, for sex. Sex with me.

I kissed him everywhere, his neck, down to a nipple. I grinned when a flick of my tongue over his nipple made him hiss. It seemed he liked it, so I did it again. His hips thrust up into me as I did so, and I couldn't wait anymore, I had to touch him. I slid down beside him, down his abdomen, down to the hard ridge of his heavy cock. Thick and long, Jake's cock was a glory in itself.

My fingers couldn't close around him, and he was much longer than the average short swift swipe. Jake required a complete stroke as I began to move my hand on him. He allowed me a moment to learn him before he put a stop to it.

"Laney, if you keep doing that, I'll come in your hand and after all of the waiting we've done, that is not where I want to come tonight."

I felt my own eyes go wide at the admission. I had power here, power to give pleasure, to make him lose control. I breathed in deep and pulled my hand away. I brushed around on the duvet until I found the foil covered condom. I quickly had the condom out and on his length before I straddled him once more, his cock once again caught between us.

Rather than sinking straight onto him, I wanted to hear him beg me for relief. That sudden moment of power thrilled me, and I wanted more of it. I kissed him, deep, hard, and with every bit of passion I had within me. Our mouths danced together, his hands at my hips in an attempt to hold me still, but I matched the rhythm of the kiss to the rhythm of my hips.

He moaned helplessly beneath me as I stroked him with my wet heat, and I felt my back arch in response. I wanted to give in then, I wanted to plunge down onto the throbbing length of his cock, I wanted to impale myself on him, but it wasn't right, not just yet. We'd waited so long, and now, I wanted this ride to be memorable.

I wasn't immune to the erotic pleasure of dancing on Jake's dick, or to the way he pressed into my clit every time my hips swirled on him, and my own breath was ragged by the time he pulled his lips from mine and buried my face in his shoulder.

"Enough Laney, please," he said in a hoarse voice. "You're torturing me."

I grinned in satisfaction and sat up, forcing my shoulders up when he tried to hold me still.

I took him in hand and held him still as I slowly

started to sink down onto him. One inch, then two, I closed my eyes and savored each one. By the time I was down to seven, Jake was trembling beneath me. I opened my eyes to see his jaw clenched into stone, and his eyes were tightly shut.

"You're a witch, casting a spell on me, aren't you?" He didn't open his eyes, he just waited, patiently as he let me have my way.

I slid down the last few inches with a dip of my hips. I had taken all of him, every last inch of him, and he was mine.

I reveled in the way he stretched me, in the way he filled me for only a breath of a moment before I braced myself with one hand against his thigh. Slow and shallow, I started to grind up and down Jake's cock, his hands guiding me with a tight grip on my thighs until we found the rhythm that had us both panting. It wasn't soft and gentle, the way I'd imagined. This was pure raw need, and soft and intimate wouldn't cut it. This had to be deep and dirty, for both of us.

Hard, fast, and deep, I rode Jake mercilessly, not letting up at all, not even when he tried to flip me. I clamped my thighs around him and stopped until he relaxed beneath me.

I needed this moment and he let me have it.

I started once more, until I was lost in him, until we were lost in each other, until my walls gripped at him with sensual glee and milked him into following me. We were both lost, but right there with each other as our bodies exploded together. I felt him shaking beneath me, and it only made me clamp down harder on him as my back arched and my head went back and my long hair teased at his thighs in total abandon.

I cried out his name just as he gasped out mine, his hands gripping my breasts in a way that suggested he needed to know I was real. My hands covered his as the ripples started to fade away, my chest heaving from my exertion.

He pulled me down to him after a moment and we clung together. We breathed together, fast and hard, shallow and quick, and finally, slow and soothing.

"I might die," he said, and I knew what he meant.

"I might join you."

"At least we'll go happy."

His hands in my hair soothed me, and then I didn't know anything else, only sweet darkness.

CHAPTER FOURTEEN

JAKE

We had several days of peace and quiet and one shopping trip at a local strip mall for clothes that we rarely wore before we had to go back home. The landline in the cabin started to ring and I looked at Laney with dread.

"I have to go. Apparently, the ads have started, and I have to go for publicity shots and interviews to help build the hype." She was cradled in my arms. Her lips still tasted like the rum and cola she'd had with dinner.

"I hate this, Jake." She'd taken so long to respond I almost thought she was asleep. She'd said she wasn't much of a drinker earlier, but she'd learned to love rum mixed with cola.

"I'm guessing as much as I do. It has to be done though. Otherwise, they'll hound me into the grave." I stroked a finger down her cheek in an attempt to get her to open those beautiful eyes of hers.

"They're going to try and force you to choose Arabella, aren't they?" She turned her head away, her voice breathless in a way that made my chest ache.

"They can't really make me do that, Laney. Besides, you know I'd never do that to you. There are some things I can't tell you, some things I can't reveal, but I can make you this promise. There's no other woman I want in my life and there's not a soul who can replace you."

I knew I loved her, though I could only express that through actions until this whole farce was over. She had to know she was my choice. I hoped it was crystal clear by now.

"When do you have to leave?" she asked, her voice strong once again as she sat up in bed, unabashedly letting the sheet fall to reveal her luscious body.

"In the morning. I'll take you home before I head to the airport. I want to leave with your scent on my skin." It was too poetic, but it was the truth.

"Alright. Christmas Eve is only a week away. We can do this, Jake. A week, and then it's over." She gave me a brave smile, and I knew we would be alright.

That was one of the things I loved about Laney. "You're always so strong, Laney. You keep my head on straight for me."

She bent over to kiss me where I was propped against the pillows and cupped my cheek. "That's because I have you to keep my head on straight, buddy."

I pulled her over me and she laughed with glee. I couldn't wait to come back to the pure happiness that only Laney had to offer me. Would it be the same after the show was over? I knew it would for me, but would it for her?

"You'll have a heavy load once school starts back." I broached the subject of her law degree. She'd told me about her plans and I admired how she wanted to be an advocate for children and the elderly.

"We can get through that too, Jake. I'll be done soon, then I'll have to dive into the real world, but we can do it. I'll have you there to help make sure I do."

"You will, after all the work you've put into it, you deserve a chance to see it happen." She ran slim fingers through my hair and smiled.

"I'm so glad you feel that way. I've always wanted to make a difference in the world." Laney's smile wavered for a moment. "After what you said about your parents, about how they died, well, I want to be someone they would appreciate, you know? Someone they'd be proud to have with their son."

"They'd be proud of you anyway, Laney. Only morons don't fall at your feet." I found my hands in her hair this time, silky copper strands that fascinated me.

I wasn't avoiding the subject of my parents or deflecting. Laney just took away some of the pain and made it possible to think about them without the threat of depression sweeping over me. She knew about the fire, about how I'd almost died with them, and she'd made it possible to talk about because I felt so calm around her. She really was my miracle savior.

"Come on, I think there's more macaroni salad in the fridge." She was deflecting, I thought with a laugh, as she jumped out of bed.

"Fine, if macaroni salad is better than sex with me, let's eat." I pushed the covers away and stood up, a pair of sleep pants covering my nudity as we walked out to the kitchen.

"It's not that macaroni salad is better than sex with you," she said with a laugh over her shoulder, "but it's necessary to keep up with you; you wear me out!" She paused long enough to give me a kiss and I knew it was moments like this that I would miss the most once I was gone.

I really didn't know how I was going to get through the upcoming week of hell.

* * *

LIGHTS WENT off in sparks and bursts. Reporters screamed out questions I couldn't or didn't want to answer. I tried not to hide my eyes from the flash of cameras as I walked out of yet another studio from an interview with yet another woman that would have been screaming sexism if I had dared to ask her the same questions she felt perfectly fine with asking me.

It was starting to wear me down and I'd only been at it for three days. I hated the probing questions, hated the lights and the show's demands even more. Most of all I hated not sleeping next to Laney. I gave an aloof but sexy gaze to the cameras; I'd studied and practiced the "gaze" Carol had insisted I perfect, until I could do it in my sleep. It hadn't distracted me from the fact that I missed Laney's laugh, the way she'd come up behind me and wrap her arms around my waist and hold me tightly, skin to skin.

I finally moved out of the lights and into a car soon after the black car drove up to the curb to take me back to my hotel. At least it was a decent hotel. I'd seen David once, as I was being shuffled to another interview, but I hadn't spoken with him yet. Trent, on the other hand, was nowhere in sight.

My head pounded out a rhythm in time with the tires on the car by the time the driver pulled to a stop in front of the hotel. I got out, staggered to the elevator, and went up to my room to hide in darkness and quiet. I'd pulled the curtains on day one and hadn't opened them since.

I'd order room service after a shower, I decided. I headed into the black tiled shower and turned it on, the blast of near boiling water soothing away the tension that had given me the headache. I stood there for long moments, letting my head clear, letting the memory of that woman's insipid questions float away.

I could do this, I repeated as a mantra, Laney was the reward.

I scrubbed off and got out, the room full of steam but I didn't care. I wrapped a large bath towel around my waist, wrapped my head in another, and put on the robe provided by the hotel. This quiet time could be just as stressful as the interviews and the camera flashes. This was when I missed Laney the most. When there wasn't a soul around to distract me.

I turned on the television and picked up the hotel's menu. I found a program that would hold my attention for a little while and ordered some dinner from the menu. I wanted to email Laney, but I suspected the show might be monitoring my communications. A little paranoid of me, but I didn't want to jeopardize anything so I kept quiet.

I watched the program, my brain finally going quiet, and was asleep before I knew it.

I dreamed of Laney, of that first time, of the way her greedy little pussy sucked me deeper into her body, and how her hips slithered over me, when something tried to intrude into my sleepy version of heaven. I turned on my side and lost myself once more in the way Laney made me feel. I was between her thighs in moments, tasting her languorously, savoring every drop of her heady scent.

I could hear myself moan as her thighs clamped around my head. I loved when she did that, I knew she'd lost all control at that point and was ready to blow. Laney exploding was one of the most powerful things I'd ever witnessed, it could literally bring me to my knees in adoration.

I could hear her sighs as her stomach started to ripple and the harsh cry that signaled she was coming hard and waited for the rest of her body to shake. She completely let go when she came, she didn't hold anything back, and I glanced up her body to watch her breasts shake, and the way her head rolled back in total surrender. It was erotic, beautiful, and totally Laney.

I was waiting for that moment when burying my dick in her would set her off again, that last signal from her that would tell me the moment was right when reality intruded once more. This time, the noise didn't stop until I called out.

"Go the fuck away!" It was probably Carol again. Or... shit, room service!

I sprang out of the bed, my hair dry but standing up around my head, and ran for the door. I pulled it open, one hand on the door, one on my robe, to find Arabella standing there with her patented smirk on her face. She threw herself into my arms, her artificially inflated lips sealed to mine, and all I could do was stumble as I tried to get her off me. Camera flashes blinded me and, befuddled, I closed the door to make it stop, Arabella still clawed into me like a cat in heat.

I pushed her away as soon as the door was closed and glared at her. "What the hell, Arabella? Did you set that up?"

That's when it dawned on me that those camera flashes meant pictures. Those pictures meant papers. Papers and headline stories on news shows and websites. "What have you done?"

"Those boys are with me. Unless you hear me out, and do as I say, those pictures are going to hit every news agency in America. We'll see what your little vixen thinks about them when she sees me in your hotel, shall we? And oh, just in case, I'll make sure you end up penniless, too." She gave me a sweet smile that dripped venom. She really was little more than a snake.

"What do you want, Arabella?"

"I want you. I want you to choose me for the show, I want you to marry me, and sign a prenuptial agreement, and then I want you to give me babies, just to make sure you're tied to me for the rest of your life." Her words came out like they should be the most delightful thing I could ever hear, but instead, they made me want to vomit. On her.

I stared at her, wondering if she was greedy or insane. Or both perhaps?

"You know I'm just a computer nerd, right? I design things that you'd never be able to comprehend. I spend hours and days doing it. I'm really not that interesting." Not to a woman like her that would want to use me as her arm candy and personal bank account. Carol must have told her I was the rich one. "I'm the poor one, you know."

It was a gamble, to see what she'd give away.

"Oh, come off it, Mallory. You're one of the richest men in the world. I want in. Or I make sure the show takes it all away."

"Alright," I said simply, going to the door and opening it. "Have a nice life."

"Pardon me?" She stood there blinking like her batteries were malfunctioning and her eyelids were on overdrive.

"I said, get out." I waved my hand at the floor to show her the way.

"But, you're not really going to give up billions for that little nobody, are you?"

"I will and am. It means nothing to me now. You people have shown me exactly how much it's worth. Laney showed me what really matters in this world."

"So, you don't really want to help kids in some dust-bowl of a country get an education?" Her eyes narrowed at me and I have to admit, that thought did sting a bit.

"I made that money once, I can make it again if I have to." The thought put the steel back in my backbone.

"Fine. But you haven't heard the end of this! Believe me, Carol is going to be pissed!"

"Not as pissed as you, I imagine." I looked at the woman, wondering how she could really be seen as beautiful when everything about her was fake.

She'd taken what had once been a beautiful canvas, and nipped, cut, and stitched herself into a parody of what beauty really was. It screamed insecurity to me, and lack of faith in herself. She had to be perfect, and that meant she had to be perfect for someone else, not herself, and that's who she should always do her best for. Herself first, then maybe, somebody else.

Watching her go actually made me sad. Laney had felt she needed to deny herself to be perfect, she had to get the best grades, had to excel in her work, and had to prove she was worthy of life because that's the atmosphere she grew up in. Her parents had always been supportive, from what she said, but she knew what society expected of a girl whose mother was a leading cardiologist; absolute perfection.

Then there was Arabella. She'd had it all given to her on a platter, but it was never enough. She felt as though she was never good enough, judging by her appearance. She had to fit society's standard of beauty to find a man to support her, but if she'd put half of her energy into educating herself that she put into 'correcting her faults', she could have been supporting herself by now.

I would make more money, I decided, just to help young girls get the educations they deserved so they never had to feel like Laney or Arabella had. I know, sympathy for the devil in Arabella's case, but she was merely a product of her society. She could not be blamed for that. Even if she was a bitch.

"Hey, it's Jackson. Let me speak to my attorney, please." Damage control was high on my agenda right now. My attorney was a savvy kind of guy, and he already had a team ready for just this instance.

Publicity was our weapon right now, and my guy was going to tear these producers and the show to smithereens if they so much as peeped out a sound that sounded like sue. I was done playing. I was going to meet my contractual obligation, then this shit was done. No more hiding, no more worries.

I'd spent a lot of time talking with the man while I was stuck in this hotel and we'd formulated our defense against Carol and her cronies. They could try to take my money, but they would not win. They would never see a dime from me. I'd destroy them with their own weapon first. I clicked on the file I'd received earlier that morning, full of images that could destroy every one of those producers, directors, and whatever else might crawl out to try and sue me. It was going to blow right up in their face if they tried.

I called room service again, promising to be awake to answer the door this time, and settled back to wait for my food. This little snit with Arabella had made me hungry and I was going to enjoy every bite of it. I wasn't playing with any of them anymore. Laney and my grandmother were too important to jeopardize over people that would waste my money on diet pills and hair extensions. Not when I had plans for building schools and raising a family of my own with a children's advocate by my side.

CHAPTER FIFTEEN

LANEY

I stared at the picture on my phone screen and wanted to smash the glass into dust.

It was an email from Carol. The subject line was full of hearts and happy smiles, that should have been my first clue that something was wrong. I opened it thinking it might be important.

Now, all I could do was sit with tears pouring down my face and wait for Tony to come back with black cherry ice cream and a big bottle of rum. Yes, I was about to get stupidly drunk for the first time in my life.

"It can't be real, honey," Tony said as he came back in the house, bags in hand. He'd bought freshly baked chocolate chip cookies too, I could smell them as I followed him.

"You mean they just made it look like Arabella was wrapped around Jake's head with the magic of software?" I was being sarcastic but I couldn't help it. I was breaking apart inside.

"Maybe. Even if it is real, it doesn't mean anything. That man loves you, Laney. Even I could sense that and Tony's a hardened kind of guy, you know?" He gave me that 'and that's that' look he'd perfected long before I came along and started taking out bowls. He turned back to look at me as he put the bowls down. "Never mind, we don't need these bowls. Come on."

He grabbed two spoons, the bags, and marched me into the living room. By the time I'd dug my first bite of ice cream out of the plastic tub I was blubbering again.

"I know he loves me, and I believe him when he says he doesn't want anyone but me, but she's gorgeous, Tony!" The ice cream melted smoothly on my tongue and if I wasn't so miserable I'd have moaned.

He handed me a glass filled with rum and cola before he found his own spoon.

"So, basically, you don't trust him?" He gave me another look, one that said 'bitch, please' without actually saying the words.

"Of course, I do!" I countered, digging deeper into the ice cream. "I just have a problem with self-confidence."

"How does he make you feel?" He took his own dig at the ice cream. And me.

"Like a queen." I glared back at the dig.

"Touché! I am THE queen though, honey, don't give me that look." He patted the back of his head and went back to the ice cream.

"So you think I'm just being silly?" I sipped at my drink before I took a cookie out of the box.

"Maybe just a little. I could understand anger. Jake shouldn't have allowed himself to get into a situation like this. Sadness and mourning? Girl, you're crazy. That man would tear down the Great Wall of China with his bare hands for you."

More ice cream disappeared, and I thought about what Tony had to say.

I brought the picture back up on my phone and looked at it again. Arabella looked stunning, even from the back. The way her right foot was kicked up looked artful too. Jake, on the other hand, looked disheveled, as though he'd just woken up, and when I enlarged the picture, it looked like he was shocked and about to push her away.

The hands that had originally looked like they were pulling her closer, now looked to be pushing her away. And his hair was that tangled kind of messy that only good sex or sleep could produce. Hmmm. Had she been leaving after a session? He was in a bathrobe after all.

I put the phone down.

"I don't think we have enough rum," I said, moaning as I opened the phone once more.

"I bought two bottles. You're going to be too sick to care by the time tomorrow rolls around." He put more rum in my glass, filling the glass from half to full.

I gulped as he handed it to me. "Drink up, sweetpea. Momma's going to make it all better."

I disagreed. "My momma would tell me to stop being a ninny and eat broccoli, it's better for my heart."

"True, very true. She'd also tell you you're being silly, though. Have some faith, girl, Christmas magic, remember? Good things are coming for you. Santa told me so last night."

"Santa? You didn't sleep with a mall Santa, did you?" I stared at him shocked.

"No, my, uh, my boyfriend might have dressed up as Santa though."

He hadn't come home until early this morning. I guess Santa had quite a few gifts in his sack for Tony.

"Oh, do tell. Boyfriend now, is he?" I urged, happy for the distraction.

"I'm getting too old to play the field. Plus, you and your boring boyfriend making goo-goo eyes at each other got me thinking. It's time for both of us to settle down." He wouldn't look at me, just kept eating the ice cream on his side of the tub.

I fell back against the couch in disbelief.

"Too... old? Settle? Oh my God, did you say settle down?"

"Girl, leave me alone. I'm *trying*. I'm not making any promises, but we'll see how it goes." He looked at me, at last, and gave me a smile. "He's a lot like your Jackson, quiet, calm, and sexy as fuck!"

"I have to meet this paragon of manhood." I gave him a grin and went back for more ice cream.

"Maybe we can have a Christmas dinner here."

"We're having dinner at Jake's Gran's house," I answered automatically. I wondered if we still were.

"Of course, you are." He looked away, and I could see sadness in his eyes.

"You were invited, I just forgot to tell you."

He turned to me, his smile back in place. "Great! Do you think she'll mind if I bring a man with me?"

I knew some of the struggles Tony faced, and I'd protect him from them all if I could. He was my tiger, my bear, and sometimes he was the kitten that needed stroking to soothe him back down.

"Mrs. Mallory will not care, believe me. She'll just be happy to be feeding another mouth." The woman loved to cook, it kept her happy it seemed.

"Good. I'll call him later. If I remember to." He tilted his own glass at me in a cheer, and we both guzzled our drinks down.

"I'm going to be so sick tomorrow," I said as I stuffed another cookie in my mouth.

"Run another mile, that'll sweat it out of you." Tony

grinned happily and poured us both another drink.

"Seriously though, what are we going to do after this is all over?" I was starting to feel the rum, but didn't mind. It was taking my mind off smashing my phone into the basest of particles.

"I'm going to keep living right here, and I imagine you'll go off to live in the woods with your mountain man. Nerd. Whatever." He was teasing me again.

"Like you wouldn't love to get your hands on Jake's, ahem, wood."

"I'd let him sp... uh, you just never mind what I meant. He is fine, girl." He put the empty tub of ice cream down and broke out some other box.

Chocolate covered cherries!

"Oh boy, I am going to be sick tomorrow!" I crammed one in my mouth and let the heavenly taste soothe me.

"There's nothing better for heartache than chocolate, alcohol, and ice cream." He waved at the empty ice cream tub with his glass. "Momma knows how to fix everything."

"I guess you do." I slurred as I downed more rum and sucked at my teeth to get chocolate out of them. "What's on TV?"

I wasn't exactly sure I could concentrate enough to watch anything, but Rudolph the Red-nosed Reindeer was on and I'd be damned if I was going to miss that! A childhood favorite of my parents, the cartoon had become a family tradition that I'd yet to miss.

"Girl, you are not about to make me watch some cartoon, are you?" Tony wrinkled his nose at the program and picked up a cherry.

"Girl, I am! You just don't know good television. How could you not love Rudolph?" I asked, pushing his hand out of the box to grab a cherry before he took another one.

"I've never seen it," he said it glibly, as if it wasn't an earth-shattering revelation!

"What?" I hit pause on the DVR and looked at him. "You have *never* seen Rudolph? What non-TV having rock did you grow up under?"

"My momma didn't want us watching stuff like that. Said it was of the devil. I was never interested in it, so I haven't seen it."

"Good grief. Wait, have you seen any Christmas cartoons at all? What about Frosty? Or Charlie Brown? Any of those?"

"Laney, cartoons just freaked my momma out in general. I've never watched them."

"Okay, settle in and buckle up, because you are about to have the experience of a lifetime." I'd find them all online if I had to, but Tony was having the full-on Christmas experience. I took another slug of rum and cola and decided I'd move on to movies after the cartoons. Wasn't there one where a kid got his tongue stuck to a metal pole for a bet?

We'd finished off one bottle of rum by the time I went through the list of cartoons I wanted to show Tony and I swear I heard him sniffle at the end of Frosty, but he wouldn't admit it.

"Stop, I can't take anymore," he slurred, caught between crying and laughing. "I think I have to go to bed. I knew I was getting too old for this shit."

"I don't think we're too old, I think we're just too full of sugar. And rum. And Christmas magic." I exploded from the couch, prancing around drunkenly as Frosty started to play again.

Tony danced with me for a moment, laughter filling the house. I didn't know what the future held, or what we were going to do about our living arrangements, but I did know that Tony would be a fixture in my life until the day I died, if I had anything to say about it.

"I'm going to bed before the room starts spinning. You probably should too, Laney." He kissed the top of my head and bounced to his room. Bounced because he went down the hall like a ball hitting bumpers in a pinball machine.

I went to take a shower to wash away the salt of my tears and to wake myself up a little. I didn't feel like crying anymore, so Tony was right about that part, but I did have to think about that email some more. Carol had sent that to me on purpose. Those little hearts were like rubbing salt in a wound, just the kind of snide thing Carol would do.

I rubbed at my suddenly itchy nose with the back of my hand and wondered why my eyes were so blurry. It probably wasn't the best idea to get drunk and take a shower, but it did make me giggle as I tried to keep my balance.

I wondered what Jake was doing right now. Was he missing me as much as I missed him? I got out of the shower and wobbled through the bathroom and into my bedroom with nothing but a towel on. Tony would fuss at me about the floors, but I wasn't thinking about floors right now. I was thinking about my man.

He'd better be alone up in that hotel room. I wondered who had called the photographers as I tripped over into my bed and passed out.

CHAPTER SIXTEEN

JAKE

I stared at the barren walls of the room I'd been trundled off to after Arabella's little escapade and fumed. Carol and her goons had come to retrieve me an hour later. Carol's only words made it sound like I was a prisoner.

"You will not be allowed out of this room until the finale, do you understand? You should have listened to Arabella. To make sure you don't find a way to communicate with your little lady love, you'll be kept here. Have a good day. Someone will bring you dinner." She gave me an insincere smile before she closed the door and locked it.

I felt like a prisoner and wondered how legal this all was. I went over to the television, a stack of DVDs on top of a player, and knew I was fucked. What happened if I had to go to the bathroom?

One more day left, that's all there was, just one more day. They'd driven me around in a van for a while before it was decided I'd be taken back to the island. A plane trip, and a few hours of sitting in the van later, I was brought to this room. There was no phone, no computer, just a bed, a television with a DVD player, and another door. What was behind the door, a closet maybe?

I found some clothes, a sink, a toilet, and a shower in a tiny room behind the door. There was also a fridge with drinks and a few snacks in it. Well, at least I wouldn't be humiliated with my bathroom needs. I took a bottle of water and dug through the pile of DVDs. I settled on a long documentary I'd been meaning to watch anyway. It looked like I was going to have a lot of time on my hands.

I spent hours watching the documentary, trying not to think about what destruction Arabella and her pictures were doing. I'm sure Carol had a hand in it all. She was still trying to force me to choose Arabella over Laney, and it just wasn't going to happen. This whole thing with kidnapping me too? These people were up shit creek and didn't even know it yet.

I kicked at the lumpy mattress and glared at the windowless walls. This sucked in the truest sense of the phrase. There was nothing to do, no way to call Laney and tell her it was all a setup, and no way to defend myself. This was so much suck!

I wanted to punch the wall but decided to do pushups instead. I went through several exercises before I'd calmed down enough to sit on the bed again. I started to pace around the room, but too many sleepless nights had left me exhausted. I turned out the lights, stretched out on the bed, turned on the documentary once more, and tried to get to sleep.

Thoughts of Laney crying kept me awake. That's when I knew I truly did love Laney. Not just because she made me laugh, or because I always wanted to be with her, but because the thought of her crying filled me with rage at the same time it made me want to soothe her tears away. I've never been the kind of guy to seek out trouble, but I wasn't afraid of it either. If Arabella and Carol were men, I'd stomp them into the ground, but they weren't. I didn't hit women, ever. But I'd find a way to make them pay, because I knew—somehow—that Laney was crying.

"Fuck!" I shouted as I stood up from the bed. "Just let me out of here!"

I pounded on the door but nobody answered. I went back to the bed and kicked it, feeling totally useless. This fucking sucked!

I finally flung myself back on the bed and made

myself watch the documentary. Before long, exhaustion finally won, and I fell asleep.

I had nightmares about being trapped in the room, fire building around me, until I finally found a window hidden behind one of the walls. I was about to climb out when I heard Laney screaming for my help.

I ran through the room once more, following the sound of her voice, but every time I thought I'd found her, the location of her voice moved. I kept running and running until I was exhausted, and slumped against the window, too tired to even climb out. Laney's voice still called to me, and I didn't have the energy to stand up and find her, to save her!

I woke up the next morning angry and not in a very good mood. Somebody had to pay for this total farce. The video diary guy came to see me early, and I glared at him, unable to hide my anger.

"Wait, you're looking a little shiny. Makeup!"

I had to sit and wait for a makeup artist to apply powder and fluff out my eyebrows before the video diary finally started.

"So, what you been up to?"

His monotone voice just irritated me more. "None of your business," I said.

"Fine. Any idea who you've chosen yet?" He bounced on one foot, obviously ready to go.

"Also none of your business."

"Right, we're sulking this morning. Fine. I'm done." He scuttled off and Carol came in to take his place.

"Hi there, handsome." She gave me a conspiratorial wink and I clenched my fists at my sides. "You all ready for the big night? I think you know what's expected of you, don't you?"

"Of course, I do," I growled at her, not caring that she flinched and stepped back.

"Good. Glad to see you're so biddable, at last." She came up to me and looked at me. "If you'd done what I asked to begin with, none of this would have happened."

"I'm sure. How much longer until this is over?"

"About six more hours. We're going to start shooting as soon as it's gone dark. We need to get a bit of film from the girls, then the big finale, some shots of all the losers crying, then you'll get to go home with your princess. She deserves it too, after what you've put her through."

I didn't scream, or punch the wall, though I really wanted to, I just gave a slight shake of my head and let her go on. I stopped listening. After what I've put Arabella through? Didn't she mean Laney? Laney had put up with shit from both of these women and was still putting up with it, if I guessed right.

I was going to play by their rules, I'd decided. I was going to do what I was told. Then, I'd do what the fuck I wanted and hope I could pick up the pieces later. At least until I was off this island and had fulfilled my part of the contract.

I stared at Carol, her voice droning on, but I didn't hear her words. That dream haunted me, the fire an obvious memory of my past, but a new element had been added; my inability to save Laney from pain and fear. I'd felt so helpless when I woke up, so angry that I'd had to shut it all down just to get through this day without killing anyone.

It was a technique I'd learned after my parents died and the grief had begun to overwhelm me. Just shut it down and get through the day. That's what I was doing now, just getting by. Carol patted my cheek for some reason, her touch making me cringe both internally and externally, and I had to fight the urge to vomit as she left.

A few more hours. I could do it. Someone came in to bring me breakfast and I ate it without paying it any attention. Someone brought me clothes and shoes, a tuxedo and black patent leather shoes, and I left them on the bed until it was time. I took another shower, dried my hair, shaved, and waited.

I was planning out the best way to use my money on education for children, when someone popped their head in. David!

"David, thank God, somebody to talk to!" I pulled him into the room and he sat on the bed with me.

"What's going on? Why do they have you in here? Kelly said there was some really bad stuff going down, but this looks like a prison! Is it because of those pictures with Arabella? Man, I got to tell you, Kelly is so mad at you!"

"Damn, they got out then?" That was not the news I wanted to hear.

"The pictures of you and Arabella wrapped around each other like melting licorice sticks? Oh yeah, they did! And Kelly wants your, as she so eloquently put it, balls for those pictures."

"It was all staged, David! Arabella came to my room. How she even knew where I was staying I can only speculate, but she threw herself at me and cameras started flashing around us. She made all these threats and then Carol came and hauled me off here. One minute a tolerable hotel, the next an intolerable prison." I waved my hand around to indicate the sparse room.

"The room does suck, Jake, I have to admit. How did you not break the door down?" He looked at it and I laughed.

"It's solid metal, David. I wasn't getting through that with my bare hands." I'd have tried otherwise. Without a second thought, I'd have torn that door down, but there had been no way I was getting through that door.

Judging by the shine on the hardware, it was brand new. I guess that's why they had me sitting outside for so long, to prepare this room and install that door. Bastards. I clenched my fists once more and looked away from David. He was studying the door, trying to figure out how to science his way through it, I'd bet.

"I see. No, I suppose you weren't. At least it's almost done." He seemed nervous now and pushed at the air on his nose.

"Do you think you'll go back to glasses when this is over?"

"It depends on whether Kelly minds them or not. If she does, I'll keep the contacts in."

"Laney is just so adorable with her glasses on." I let slip before I realized what I'd said.

"You've seen her with glasses? When?" He looked at me, lost.

"She had them on one day... probably the same day you talked to Kelly about how mad she was at me." I let my words trail off in a mutter as he caught my meaning. He'd been in contact with Kelly after we'd all been sent home. Just like Laney and me. I grinned at him and he pushed air up the bridge of his nose once more.

"Ah, yes, well. Okay then. Well, I just wanted to see you before the show. Good luck. I know I've chosen Kelly. I haven't seen Trent, or Skip for that matter. Are you choosing Laney? Kelly will kill you if you don't!" His cheeks had flamed red for a moment before he stood and turned away from me.

I looked at him, wondering if he was really curious or if he was spying.

"I'll do what everyone expects me to do," I responded.

"That could be anything, Jake. Follow your heart, isn't that what you told me?" He clapped me on the shoulder before he left and I took a deep breath. He hadn't been spying then, just curious. I felt bad for even wondering now.

He'd probably tell me it was the intelligent thing to wonder anyway. You could never tell in contests like this.

I could do this. I had to.

I dressed in my tux when prompted and followed the man out that came to get me as the time rolled near.

I could hear the women in the other part of the house and knew the time had come to do what was right. Even if I wanted to climb the stairs, go through every room until I found Laney, and run out of the house with her, I had to do the right thing right now, and that meant heading in the opposite direction, so that's what I did.

Cameras were still being set up in the foyer and the set designer was running around in a panic. Somehow the roses that adorned every surface were wrong and she hated them and was on the verge of suicide. "They won't show up as well on camera! How could you order the wrong color, you idiot?"

She was screeching at some underling and I felt sorrier for them than I did the designer. People only glanced at that stuff, the roses weren't so important that she should be in such a panic. Was everybody in this business an infantile butthole, or was it just the staff for this show?

I left the woman now in tears and walked to the same area where we'd started from and stood in the spot marked for me. People rushed by, none paying any particular attention to me. Only the set was important at the moment. I watched it all, hating every moment of it, but determined to see this through properly. I had to.

Memories played in my mind as I stood there, waiting for the others to appear in this farce of a show. Only a few weeks ago I'd watched Laney come down those stairs and fell in love for the very first time. Her eyes had sparkled they were so full of laughter and irreverence. I knew then she wasn't taking any of it seriously, much like me. She'd fascinated me from the start. Sure, she was breathtaking in her gown, and she had the most amazing eyes, and damn! All of that red hair! That wasn't what caught my eye though, it was how she looked so beguilingly amused that got me.

I knew she wasn't here for wealth. Tony had signed her up for the show in collusion with my grandmother.

What had started out as whim had turned into something far more serious. Now, I had to make a decision that could throw it all away.

Calm, cold, collected, I reminded myself as I waited. Do what's right, do what you have to do. Get through this. Then pick up the pieces.

I grimaced and clenched my jaw. I could do it. I had to, right?

I felt my knees go weak as a new thought occurred to me. After those pictures, would Laney even bother to show up tonight?

CHAPTER SEVENTEEN

LANEY

How could a hangover last two days? I'd woken up from the Christmas cartoon fest with the idea I might not actually be alive. I might have wondered more if the painful headache and extreme nausea hadn't convinced me I was alive, if barely. Not doing that again, ever.

I'd slept most of the day, not caring that I should be packing, that I should be working up an extreme case of anxiety, and totally not thinking about Jake kissing Arabella dressed in nothing more than a bathrobe. I slept and woke up for water a few times, before going straight back to sleep.

When I woke up the second day, I didn't quite feel like I was on the verge of complete organ failure, but the nausea was still there.

When a car showed up in the driveway, I was ready. I had a small case packed, a pair of large sunglasses firmly in place, and the conviction that I could get through this day without tears ensconced in my brain. Mainly, my brain was still too numb to function so I felt like a zombie as I got on the plane and then landed.

The noise inside the house started a low throb just behind my eyes, and even Kelly's exuberant greeting could do little to bring me back to life.

"I've missed you so much!" Kelly cried out as she wrapped me in a bear hug.

I'd only just made it to my room when she'd found me, and now, I wanted nothing more than to get into that bed and sleep the rest of my hangover off. I could see her features droop in disappointment at my muttered 'hey', though, so I tried to work up just a little enthusiasm.

"I've missed you too, honey, I'm just not feeling well." It wasn't a lie, I felt like that stain you find on sidewalks sometimes, the one you avoid because you don't know what it is or how long it's been there, but it's still too gross to contemplate.

"Aw, you've picked up a bug! Or is it nerves?" She looked at me with concern, and I envied her how fresh and happy she looked.

I'd showered that morning, but I still felt like I was a walking vector for the plague.

"Hangover. My BFF decided I needed to get drunk

two days ago and I agreed with him. Until the next day, that is." I gave her a weak smile.

"You saw them then?" Anger flashed in her eyes, and I nodded in confirmation.

"Yeah. I saw the pictures if that's what you mean." I pushed into my old room and sat on the bed I'd used. "It'll be alright. Whatever happens, it will be alright. I'm not giving up, I know the whole thing was probably staged, but something tells me Jake wasn't in on it."

"I'm sure you're right. Listen, we're supposed to be in makeup and hair in twenty minutes. Do you want me to wait for you?" Her voice was gentle and kind, and I loved her for it.

"If you want to. If you want to go spying for glimpses of David, that's fine too. I can meet you there."

"I'll just wait with you. I have a lifetime of seeing him, I hope." She gave me a wink that said she knew good and well she did and I smiled, I couldn't help it.

"This is going to be a long day, isn't it?" I wanted coffee and something to eat, but then felt my stomach roll at the thought of food. Alright, maybe just coffee.

"More than likely."

"Can you believe it's Christmas Eve?" I asked, both of us sitting on the bed, staring out of the window.

"I can't, no. This is all just so weird." She waved her hand around. "I signed up for this on a whim, and it's changed my life so much in such little time. It's kind of overwhelming, isn't it?"

"It is. A lot, actually. I've never really been in love before, and now I can't seem to get away from it." I let the air blow out from my cheeks as I thought about it. "He'd better not mess this up, that's all I have to say."

"What will you do if he chooses Arabella? I know they've put him under a mega amount of pressure to do it." Her eyes probed my features, looking for an honest answer.

"I really don't know. I don't know if they're going to cut and paste this all together, how they're going to try and make us all look. Maybe I'll barely get a minute of airtime, but it'll be hugely humiliating, won't it?" I paused to think about it. "More than that, though, it will break my heart. Even if it is fake and he came and asked me to go out with him, choosing Arabella will mean I can't trust him, won't it?"

"I think that's a really tough choice to have to make. For both of you, and I don't envy you at all, right now." She shook her head, those red curls bouncing around her head. "I think you're both in a tough spot."

"You're right. There's so much going on that we aren't told about, and we all know these stupid shows end up in divorce. None of it's real, and as soon as the real world intrudes, attitudes change. Faults that weren't exposed come to light."

I could see I'd hurt Kelly with my thoughtless words, and I rushed to comfort her. "Oh honey, I didn't mean to hurt you! I'm sure you and David will be fine, we can all see you're both soul mates. I was just trying to talk myself into not being so hurt if Jake chooses Arabella over me. I'm so sorry."

She gave me a wobbly smile that soon straightened. "You're right, Laney. We don't know what's going to happen in the future, but I can tell you this. Jake really does adore you. It's written all over his face the moment you walk into a room."

"I guess that's why I'm not really worried. That and the hangover. I know Jake." I stopped before I revealed too much. I'm sure there were cameras in here too.

"I think you do. Come on, let's head down to torture chamber A."

I laughed, the makeup and hair room was very much like a torture chamber.

An hour later we both emerged, hair done in another elaborate upsweep with a million pins and enough hairspray to ensure that even after the pins were out our hair would not move, and our makeup was expertly applied. We were herded into another room, torture room B, where our dresses were hanging on dress forms. I stopped in my tracks and my heart thudded to a stop for a full second.

Wedding dresses!

What kind of bullshit was this?

"Oh my God, look at mine, Laney!" Kelly ran to the one with her name on it, an A-line confection in ivory silk and lace that would suit her perfectly.

I looked at the dresses and couldn't help but think what a cruel joke this was. Whoever wasn't chosen would look like a jilted bride and the audience would eat it up. With a deep breath and a sigh, I walked up to mine. I could do this. I had to.

I touched the crisp white lace of a classic ball gown, a sweetheart neckline made modest with a lace overlay that formed the shoulders and sleeves. It was really beautiful and the butterflies flitting down each side to leave the middle bare really was breathtaking. This was not a cheap gown. It was the kind of princess gown I might have chosen myself when the time came.

I just stared at it and reality finally intruded. Jake very well might humiliate me tonight. Then again, he might make my dreams come true. Either way, it would all be over soon. I just had to get through this part.

"Oh my God, I'm going to look so beautiful for Jake!"

I heard that voice and knew who it was before I even glanced around.

Arabella, in all of her dark beauty, was there with her hands to her mouth, faux shock mingled with even more faux tears as she stared at the silk slip that was meant to be her gown. It looked more like an ivory nightgown, silky and shimmery, designed to fit her frame perfectly. She was already shuffling off her clothes and putting on the lingerie set out for us.

By the time she was in hers, I was barely able to get my corset on. An assistant had to come and help me tie the back up. She was right, though, she did look perfect in her gown. You couldn't even tell she had undergarments on they all lay so flat. I tried not to look at her, to wish I had a gown like that, but I did steal the occasional glance. I stepped into my own and heard gasps all around the room. There were five of us left, and each had an assistant, so 9 gasps filled the air, and one snarky hmph. I didn't have to look around to see who that was from.

The assistant had placed a frail-looking tiara on my head as a finishing touch and I looked around the room.

"You really were meant to be a princess," I heard my assistant say. I looked around and saw confirmation in the eyes of everyone but Arabella.

"Thanks, you're all beautiful too, you know?" I meant it too.

We were all taken out one by one to do a final interview before we were paraded out for the men and it was finally my turn.

The same droll little man with his camera and monotone voice greeted me in a room paneled in white and dark wood. A single ornate chair sat in the room, red velvet and gold paint made the chair look royal.

"What do you think is going to happen tonight?" he started, abrupt as usual.

"I think some hearts are going to break and others will soar." Poetic, but it was how I saw it.

"Right. And your heart?"

"My heart will…" I paused, lost for words. I looked around uncomfortably, but nothing came. "My heart will be fine."

"Noncommittal and boring. Do you want to try again?" He had the bored look down to perfection.

"No." I could do bored too, my lifted eyebrow said.

"Fine. When Jake chooses Arabella, I mean *if*, will you be disappointed?" He looked at me this time with hope, hope that his question had stung.

I gave him nothing. "Jake's choice is his choice. It's not over yet."

"God, I hate my job. Fine. Send the next one in."

I smirked a bit as I got up, but the dress made standing difficult. Once up, I left the room and went down the hall where the rest of the girls were sitting. Kelly was there, her hands nervously twisting in her lap.

"I'm so terrified I'm going to fall down those damned stairs!" She said, indicating the stairs just ahead of us with a nod of her head.

"Me too. Just bunch your gown in your hand until

you're down, the weight of these things should pull out any wrinkles that form." The bottom of Kelly's dress was bedazzled with silver ornaments and sparkled lace.

For a moment, I wondered if the person who'd chosen the dresses had made the choice of each with those possibilities in mind. Surely not, I told myself, my head tilted as I considered the stairs. Killing your contestants wasn't a good idea, after all.

At last, the final woman came out and sat down beside me. Arabella.

"They saved the best for last, you know," she said as she sat down beside me, carefully wiping at the corner of her mouth. Her hair was different too, I finally noticed, some kind of sultry Lauren Bacall waves.

"I'm sure they did, sweetie," I said, with a pat of her hand. From the glare she gave me, I knew she'd understood my patronizing statement.

"We'll see who's so smug in a little while, won't we?" she sneered at me, her pretty face an ugly mask of hate.

"Why do you hate me so much, Arabella? Don't you think it's a little crazy how you've taken such a dislike to me? I've not done a thing to you." I was genuinely curious. "I mean, I know it's a competition, but you're just so full of hate!"

The thought made me shudder, how full of her own hate she was. It must be making her miserable. She just glared at me again, her brain obviously working overtime.

"I play to win. You shouldn't be a threat, but Jake is nothing more than a stupid man, so I guess a red-headed bimbo could turn his head. Anyway, it's almost done now. I know who he's going to choose, and you'll be the one crying into your pillow tonight." She blanched at the last and I knew she'd given away more than she'd planned to.

She stuck her nose in the air after that, and I looked past her to see the windows revealed a dark sky. It was time.

From below I heard the music start, and my heart started to pound. This was it. The moment where my life changed once again. For better or worse.

I stood as the women ahead of me stood and followed along, my brain going to autopilot for the moment. One foot in front of the other, one foot in front of the other, that was the pattern I followed as I edged my way to the stairs. Before I knew it, I was at the top, looking down into Jake's beautiful green eyes.

Our eyes locked, and I forgot my worries and really smiled for the first time since he'd left me. It was okay, it was going to be fine, now that I could see him, now that I knew he really was real. My Jake, in living color.

He didn't take his eyes off me once he'd spotted me. He looked enthralled and in love. I could see it all over his face. I came down the stairs on a cloud of happiness and stood in the position marked out for me. I kept my head held high, and a smile was plastered on my face. He would not let me down.

And then he looked at Arabella and my world started to crumble. He looked defeated, and I knew it was over. I tried to keep the smile on my face, but it was hard. So very hard when he looked like the world had just ended. Nausea hit me hard and fast and I gulped as I tried to calm my stomach. Not now, please not now.

CHAPTER EIGHTEEN

JAKE

"Clear!" A voice called out and I knew the cameras were off. I turned away, my hand over my mouth as I saw Laney turn away, her face blanched with realization.

"Stay exactly where you are, right now, do not move, do not twitch a muscle!" Carol called out to us from the landing at the stairs. "I will remind you, this is being broadcast live, so please, no swearing when the cameras come back on, people!"

I'd forgotten that part. I scrubbed at the back of my neck with my hand, my gaze on the floor now. I couldn't watch Laney and do what I needed to do.

I glanced up to see Carol glaring down at me menacingly. I wanted to give her the finger but held myself back. It wouldn't accomplish anything if I did.

With a sigh, I turned back to face the music, the women, my fate. Laney wouldn't meet my eyes. Hers were cast down to the ground, hands clasped behind her back. She'd looked so amazing as she came down those stairs in that wonderful gown. She looked like the princess I wanted to make her, the kind that could get down and dirty in the mud, and the kind that could wear designer labels with just as much ease. I wanted to give her the world at her feet, and seeing her like this I knew she deserved it. She deserved everything I could give her with my love and my money.

But I might lose the second part if I chose the first part. My eyes darted to Arabella and I knew what hatred was. She gave me a saucy wink and my hands clenched again. She made me feel so helpless and frustrated, the furthest thing from love there was. How could she take such delight in that torture?

How could one person be so bitter? I wondered as the cameras came back on and Skip walked into the room.

"It's that time, folks, time for decisions to be made and for lives to change. Tonight, we're going to learn who the fellas have picked as their mate, and we'll also reveal which of these rather handsome gentlemen is going to give his lady the life of her dreams."

He wandered in front of Trent, mic in hand, and eyed the man up and down. "Have you made a decision, Trent?"

"I have, Skip, and it's going to be a shocker, I think."

Trent started to move but Skip stopped him.

"Don't tell me yet, just wait a minute. Down, fella, don't be so eager." Skip winked at the camera and moved to David.

"And you, David? Our gentle soul with the spirit of a poet, have you made your choice?"

"I have, Skip," David said plainly, giving nothing away.

"Are you anxious to reveal your choice?" Skip asked, a rather silly question if you asked me.

"I'll be happy to get back to my normal routine, and I hope she accepts my choice, because I think she'll be the perfect addition to my life, Skip. An amazing woman, she really is." David winked back at Skip.

I stared at David in shock. Love really did change a man! Our serious David, always so quiet, had a playful side I'd never seen from him before!

"And what about you, Jake? I've heard you've had some difficulty making your choice." Again, a toothsome grin and a wink for the camera. The man was incorrigible.

"I've come to the best decision I can, Skip. The only one I can possibly make really."

"Good to hear, good to hear. Now..." Skip swung around to the ladies before he could go on. "Onto the ladies. Wow, you're all so gorgeous, my dears. How are you? Ready to get on with this?"

We all nodded in agreement and Skip moved to the middle ground between us all.

"Now, gentlemen, I think it's time we put our ladies and the audience out of their misery, don't you?" He winked at us this time. I wanted to punch the man if he didn't get on with it.

"David? Are you ready to reveal your choice?" Skip turned to David and waited.

I heard a squeak out of David and had to smother a chuckle.

"I am, Skip." He was finally able to answer, his eyes already on the beaming Kelly.

"Then, please, reveal all to us now." Skip dramatically flourished his hand in the direction of the women and David walked straight over to Kelly.

"Kelly, if you'll have me, I want you to be my choice and my bride." David went down on one knee as Kelly squealed and jumped with happiness, the music swelling dramatically around us.

"Yes, David, oh my God, yes!" She dragged him from his knees and a rather dramatic kiss began. Skip had to clear his throat to get them to stop.

"Well, there we go, folks, a rather dramatic turn of events there. Let's see what our next bachelor can bring to our show. Jake, have you made your choice?" He turned to me with hard eyes and I froze.

Why didn't they ask Trent first? I glanced at Laney

and saw she didn't look well at all. My heart broke for her, but I knew that it would soon be over. I straightened my back and chin and looked directly at Skip.

"I have, Skip. It wasn't a hard choice, really." I glanced up and saw Carol glaring down at me like an evil monkey and gave her a wink of my own. "I made up my mind a long time ago."

I took my first step, a step toward Arabella, and carried on. She looked so damned smug, her head tilted in triumph, waiting for my kiss.

"Arabella," I started, "you are one beautiful woman, there's no doubt about that."

I stood in front of her and took her hand. I heard a noise from Laney, but forced myself to ignore it. "You would make any man proud to have you on his arm. Your beauty is perfection, and you really should be on the cover of magazines."

She pranced in place, accepting her due as queen of the ball as the music began to swell once more.

"But, inside, you're a mess. And rather ugly." She looked up at me, shocked into total silence. "Laney, on the other hand…"

I dropped the witch's hand and moved to Laney. She looked so sick and I felt terrible about what I'd just done. Her eyes were wide, and she looked a little green around the edges. I had to fix this, quickly.

"Laney, you are perfection inside and out. I've never

had a single doubt about you. Not even once. I choose you, if you'll have me."

I heard a screech of rage from Carol and Arabella, but it was Laney that had my attention. Her eyes went impossibly wide, her face flushed, and before I could do anything, she turned her head and vomited all over Arabella.

"You bitch, oh my God, oh my GOD!" Arabella screamed, her hands up to protect her face, and honestly, I couldn't blame her. Being vomited on had to be one of the most humiliating things to happen to a person. It was also hilarious to watch.

Laney let go several times before she finally crumpled into a heap of tears on the floor. People finally started to scramble around and I heard a voice screaming 'clear' as people crawled out of the woodwork to clean up the mess and one hunkered down in front of Laney.

I heard cell phones going off all over the place, and all I could do was laugh. I sat with Laney after we moved her out of the view of cameras and held her hand as she cried.

"I puked all over Arabella. God, I'm going to die of humiliation." She leaned her head against my shoulder and blew into a tissue as tears continued to pour down her face.

"You might, but I'll be there to revive you." I chucked

her under the chin and pulled her face up. "You still haven't answered me.

"That was a rotten thing you did, Jake!" She glared at me, but gratefully took a piece of gum from a passing assistant. She chewed for a minute before she continued. "You know I can't say no to you."

"I was rather hoping you couldn't."

I could hear cheering from the other room and looked up to see David and Kelly were the culprits, along with quite a few of the staff. Carol glared at us.

Arabella was assisted out of the foyer and into another room. Somebody had mopped up the floor and now the cameras were preparing to go back on.

"Do you think you'll be in trouble?" Laney asked, her eyes on me as Trent made his choice. Neither of us really cared about who he chose. We knew it was a sham anyway. Trent and Skip had been carrying on an affair throughout the whole show.

"I don't care. Really, I don't. I'll take care of Gran, I'll find a way to do that. And you, although I don't think you're that kind of a woman, are you?" I looked down at her and saw a fierce pride burning in her gaze.

"No, I'm not that kind at all. I don't care if you have more money than the US gross domestic product. I only want you, Jake, not your money. You know that." She looked at me tenderly, her gaze full of only love.

I wanted to carry her away now, I wanted to take her

back to the cabin in the woods and make love to her until neither one of us could move, but I knew there was one more part to the show. The big reveal.

"You will get back out there, and you will smile. Go!" Arabella came out of the room, Carol behind her. She'd changed and been cleaned up, but her hair and makeup were still a mess. She was being made to go on national TV looking like that, just another humiliation. One she deserved, I felt.

"Do you feel up to it, or shall I carry you in, Laney?" I asked, fully meaning it.

"I can walk. I feel so much better now."

She gave a quiet laugh and we stood up together. An assistant had given her a chair and she sat down as the cameras moved around. First, they panned over the women that hadn't been chosen and then over the winners.

"Are you feeling better, Laney?" Skip asked, coming to her immediately.

"Much, Skip, thank you. Sorry, Arabella," she called out the apology over her shoulder.

"Now, Trent and David have their lady fairs, but what about you, Jake? Have you accepted him, Laney?" Skip gave an excited wiggle of his eyebrows and waited.

"I have, Skip."

"Congratulations!" the other man cried, his eyes happy.

"Now, it's time to reveal the final secret and the prizes of the show!" Skip turned back to the camera. "One of our fellas is a billionaire. The question is, which one is it?"

I could see the camera panning over all of us and tried not to grin. I guess Laney already knew, but I was still excited. I could finally tell her everything, there would be no more half-truths, no more deflection, just the total honest truth. If I didn't get sued into prison, anyway. My lawyer had that sorted, I hoped. There was more than one way to fry a fish, after all.

"Kelly, who do you think it is?" Skip pounced and held the mic in front of Kelly.

"Oh. I think it's Jake. David has to be the teacher."

"Ah, wise observation." Skip's eyebrows wiggled again.

"And you, sweetheart?" I could tell Skip had already forgotten her name.

"I think it's Trent. He's just so handsome and funny." She twirled his hair in her fingers and for a moment I was worried we were going to have another case of spontaneous vomiting on the set. Skip got himself under control, thankfully.

"And you, Laney? You've heard what the others have to say, who do you think is our most eligible bachelor of all?" Skip waited for Laney to speak.

She looked at me for a moment and then smiled.

"I don't care really, Skip. It could be any of them. Money doesn't give you a look or a smell. There's no way to identify a rich person from a poor one when they all dress the same."

I liked that.

"Of course, but an answer would be nice, just for our audience."

"I think it's Trent. He's always going on about his past and how he was raised. I'd have to guess it was him. I think Jake might very well be the plumber, he's good with his hands, you know."

"Then you'd be wrong, my dear." Skip popped up and gave the camera yet another wink. "Because our real rich man is the one you're sitting beside! A tech giant, Jackson Mallory is a god among men. He's also a philanthropist that gives to many aid groups and has plans to provide education to the needy in some rather amazing ways."

I saw her eyes go wide and knew she was impressed, but I still didn't think it had quite soaked in yet. I was a billionaire and not just a little one.

I heard Arabella whimper in the background and my grin broadened.

"And just to ease the tension, David is the plumber, a very successful one with his own chain of businesses and Trent is the teacher."

"I knew he wouldn't be able to stand in front of a

classroom of students." I heard Laney mutter and chuckled.

"It's an odd job for a poet, though, isn't it?" I leaned over and asked her, ignoring the rest of Skip's banter for a moment.

"Not really, most of the time he won't be around people and he has time to think as he works. I imagine it keeps him busy too."

She gave me a happy smile and Skip drew our attention once more.

"Now for the prizes. Each of the contestants will be receiving $100,000, a new car worth $40,000, and a trip to Hawaii, also on us."

I heard Laney gasp in excitement at last.

"I can pay off the rest of my education!" she whispered to me.

"I'm giving mine to my charitable foundation. It can always use more money." I made the decision on the spot. "The car I'll give to someone who needs it."

"But then you won't have any prizes at all!" Laney said, her brows knitted.

"I'll have you, Laney. That's all I need." I pulled her hand up, wrapped around my own, and kissed her fingers.

"I guess you're right." She smiled happily and I knew that this was only the beginning for us.

CHAPTER NINETEEN

LANEY

We took a helicopter straight to the cabin in the woods, my second flight of the day, but this time, I was heading for a much brighter future. The helicopter was Jake's and he'd arranged one for Kelly and David as well. Trent had disappeared, along with Skip, directly after the cameras went off.

I remembered Carol's face as the helicopters landed and how she'd blustered that there would be repercussions to Jake. He'd handed her a card and cut her words off with his own, saying, "My lawyer has a few things to ask you about some kidnap charges I'll be pressing against you and the rest of the show, as well as some pictures I'm sure you'll remember if you think about it real hard."

Her mouth had fallen open when Jake winked at her and I couldn't help but laugh loudly. Oh yes, I loved this man. He'd taken care of our worries with just a few sentences.

Carol looked defeated as we flew away. I guess she was going to have a lot of explaining to do. I waved, just to rub it in. Petty, but I felt I deserved it after all the woman had put me through.

Dressed in my own clothes once more, my hair still a helmet around my head, I watched the world fall away.

Within an hour the helicopter was setting down in an area I hadn't noticed before and we were home.

Jake grabbed my hand and we ran to the house, before waving the pilot away. He gave us a waggle of his propellers before he flew away.

"Thank God, it's all over now." Jake pulled me to him as soon as we were in the house and pressed me into the door.

I'd brushed my teeth before we left and drank plenty of water, so I didn't stop him. I took his kiss and returned it with gusto, clasping my hands around his neck. I wanted his kiss, I needed it.

"Mm, it's so nice," he said once he'd pulled away, but he soon came back for some playful pecks. "I can be totally open with you now. We can make real plans."

"Yes, we can. Right now, for instance, I want a shower to get my hair back to normal, and then I want a sandwich. Then, I want you."

"Or we could mix it all up and do all of that together.

The way I plan on doing everything from now on." He kissed me again and I forgot about the shower for a moment.

His lips were stirring a new fire in me and I pressed into him, a moan vibrated my throat as his fingers traced down the length.

"Let's get you that shower." He murmured as he pulled me from the door.

I laughed and let him pull me, both of us flinging our clothes away as soon as we stepped into the bathroom. He set the water how I liked it best and pulled me in, our bodies pressed together immediately.

The jokes were gone, but I still laughed as I felt my hair go wet and slide down my back in a weird blob. "I forgot the pins."

We started to pull them out, an experience that was not painless, and we tossed them away, Jake soothing every spot he pulled a pin from with his fingers. Before long they were all out and Jake was smoothing shampoo into my hair. He gently massaged my very sore scalp and carefully worked my hair into a tangle-free mass with conditioner. He watched me as he dipped my head back into the spray, his eyes trailing from my lips to the tips of my breasts.

Game time was over. I looked at him, trust and love burning in my eyes. He reached for the soap and soaped up a washcloth before running it over my body. "You really are perfection, Laney."

He leaned down to kiss me, the cloth moving over my breasts, and down my stomach, to settle between my thighs. It soon fell away, and Jake found me with his fingers. He pulled the shower out of its holder and used it to wash the soap from my body and to direct a pulse of water at my clit.

His fingers teased me, going from my clit to dive within me, until he found a pattern that made me gasp and lean against the shower wall. I watched him, my eyes glued to his as the pulse of water and stretching pressure of two of his fingers within me made me gasp his name.

"Like that, Laney?" he asked, his lips moving towards mine slowly. "I can find something else if it's not to your liking."

His lips brushed against mine and my nipples went as hard as stone in anticipation of what else he had in mind.

"I can suck these beautiful nipples of yours, for instance." His tongue flicked against a dark rose peak and I sucked in air between my teeth at the bolt of pleasure it filled me with.

His fingers were buried within me now, the shower head set to a pulse that had my hips dancing with pure lust. I opened my eyes and watched as he took a nipple between his lips, sucked, and then set it free. He made me groan when he flattened his tongue to give me one long lick.

"Jake. Baby, please, make me come. I need you to make me come. Fuck, I need it so bad." I wasn't the least bit ashamed to ask for what I wanted. Not anymore. I knew he'd give it to me.

I heard an amused chuckle, and then my nipple was caught between his teeth, his tongue flicking at it in an incredible rhythm that was so pleasurable it was almost painful, but I never wanted him to stop. I locked my fingers into his hair and pressed his face into me, riding his fingers and the shower head as he sucked me, harder, tighter, and… fuck!

My walls clamped down on his fingers and I heard a grunt of satisfaction as Jake felt it too. I let pleasure carry me away. My hips moved against him, tempting him to join me, but I knew he would when he was ready, and only then.

He sucked my nipple impossibly tighter, and what had been satisfying became too much, it became more than just getting off, it was a spiritual experience. I stopped breathing as I climbed higher, as sensations tore through me. I didn't know it was possible for every muscle in my body to ripple like that, or to feel good while doing it, but Jake drove me on, deeper, higher, until I had to scream in a breath of air or die.

"Jake, fuck!" It was all I could say as I writhed in his arms, not even aware his hips had me pinned to the wall to keep me upright.

I couldn't think of how to describe any of it, I could only experience it, until he decided I'd had enough, and finally let me come down. His fingers left my body, the shower head went back in the holder, and he picked me up in his arms to carry me to the bed.

We fell together, our skin still soaking wet, but neither of us cared. Our lips were joined as he slid into me, bare of a condom or any other impediment. He was mine and that was all that mattered.

I accepted him gladly, my legs wrapped around his waist as he switched on the bedside light to stare into my eyes. He watched me as he stroked into me, deep and slow, his eyes avid for the sight of me. "I love you, Laney. I think I always will."

"I love you, Jake." I gave him back that gift gladly, my body moving in time with his as we forgot how to breathe once more.

My eyes closed as he stroked within me, stoking my passion once more. I reached up with my face, wanting his kiss. I bit at his bottom lip gently, wanting to feel him, to taste him. His lips sought out mine, sought out the moisture of my mouth. Our tongues tangled and swiped as they moved together.

I could feel it coming again, that unbearable pleasurable pressure. My hands went to his ass to direct his pace, to press him deeper. He moved as I directed and my nails bit into his skin in gratitude.

"That's it, baby, just like that," I panted up to him, my nails still gripping his ass, not letting him go.

I pressed my feet into the bed to get a better grip, to thrust back up to meet him as the sensation became addictive, and I couldn't have stopped if someone had screamed fire. I needed what Jake gave me, exactly like this.

I licked my dry lips, waiting for it, for that moment of more I knew was coming. He was panting my name, his lips pressed into my neck as he worked to give me just the right pressure. Then he bit into my neck in just the right spot, at just the right depth, and I was gone.

He rode out the sweet temptation of my pulsing pussy, keeping up his grind, until I could pulse no more. I fell back against the bed, totally spent. Until he pulled away.

I followed, confused, but Jake just turned me over onto my front, down onto the bed, and I grinned as he pushed my right leg up onto the bed. Oh yes, dirty time!

He lifted my hips and plunged into me once he'd found the right angle. Leaning over me, Jake pulled my hands up with one fist, his other still on my hips. I loved the feeling of control he had over me, but I also knew he would stop if I made the slightest objection. I enjoyed giving myself up to him, though, and let him take what he wanted from me.

"That's right, baby. Fuck me. Harder!" I demanded, the sweetness gone, replaced with the pure need for pleasure. "Fuck me right, baby, you know how to do it! Only you know how to do it, Jake."

He panted as he drove into me, hard and deep, and I knew he was just there, on the brink of blowing his own head off with pleasure. I squeezed the muscles of my walls, milking him from within and I heard a satisfied gasp. That had done it. He was done now.

"Laney!" He cried my name, helpless as he gave me all he had to give. I felt him pulsing within me and sighed, content that Jake was really mine as I was his. Always. Neither of us could give this up, after all. I think we'd die without it.

CHAPTER TWENTY

LANEY

A Year Later

I was dancing around the kitchen of a much larger cabin, wondering which was better, a good time with clothes on or clothes off, when I saw Tony was calling my phone. I picked it up as I put biscuits in the oven. Mrs. Mallory, now Jane to me, had started the sausage.

"You'd better hurry, breakfast will be done soon."

"Girl, I'm outside. I just wanted to give you a warning in case you had that man of yours naked again. I learned early on, remember?" I went through the house to find him smirking at me from the front door. He kissed my cheek before he came in, his eyes looking around. "I love what you've done with the place."

We'd expanded the cabin and now lived here full-time with his grandmother. I'd graduated and passed my bar exam, and we were celebrating. We had so much to celebrate, I'd tell them all just how much shortly.

"Did you get the wedding photos yet?" Tony asked me, and I picked up the album on a cabinet he'd made for us as a wedding present. "Oh, these are good."

He was flipping through the pictures taken only a few weeks ago, one of the happiest days of my life. We'd married on the beach, my parents there, and his gran. Tony, his now steady boyfriend Lane, Kelly, and David also came, along with other friends we had. It had been an amazing day of love and a night of wonder for us both.

We'd had a classic pig roasting, but we'd also had fire dancers, fireworks, and a lot of laughs. The pictures captured it all as well as the more tender moments. The moment when my mother gave me her mother's pearls to wear. The moment Jake slid his grandmother's wedding ring on my finger and I smiled at her in gratitude. The moment we'd kissed after the wedding was done. It was all there in beautiful pictures I'd cherish always.

The one of all of us staring in amazement as the fire dancers twirled their flaming batons was now hanging on the wall above the fireplace. I'd still had on my flowing lace wedding gown, far different from the one

I'd worn on the show, with my hair free and blowing in the ocean breeze, just the way Jake liked it, all of us smiling in glee. His gran and my mother had been looking at us both, their faces full of contentment. It was just too good to hide in a book and represented what mattered most to us: each other, our family, and our friends.

"Hey, baby, I've got the tickets ready now." Jake came in, a grin on his face as he bent to kiss me. "Hey, Tony, how are you, man?"

"Much better now that your friends are buying my work. Thanks for the hookup, Jake." He gave Jake a fist-bump and I went to check the biscuits.

"Y'all heading out tonight?" Jane asked, her eyes watching the sausage carefully.

"Yeah, we won't be gone long this time, Gran. It's just to pick a site." We were going to one of the islands that had suffered from a hurricane this past summer in the Atlantic. Every building had been destroyed, and we were going to use some of Jake's vast bank account to help start rebuilding.

"Well, just be sure to take mosquito repellent. I'm not sure Laney should be going down there in her condition." Jane looked at me pointedly and I gaped at her.

"How did you know?" I turned to her and hissed the words out quietly, hoping the boys hadn't noticed.

"A granny has her ways," she said mysteriously and

grinned at me before she gave me a peck on the cheek. "Tell him now."

"What are you talking about Gran? What condition, Laney?" Jake looked at me concerned and Tony just looked amazed.

"You going to give me a niece, Laney?" Tony asked quietly, his eyes hopeful.

"Yeah, I am actually," I said happily, stroking my still flat belly happily.

"What? What are you talking about, Laney?" Jake came to stand in front of me, his eyes wild with confusion. "Are you... are you pregnant?"

"I am," I responded, watching him for his reaction. I didn't have to wait long because he'd picked me up before I finished speaking and twirled me around.

"Jake, dear God, don't swing pregnant ladies around like that. It was bad enough watching her puke all over the place on live television, I don't want to see it in person!" Good old curmudgeonly Mrs. Mallory.

"A baby. My god! A baby. Should we cancel the trip, Laney? Maybe you should stay here." He looked panicked, but I put a hand to his cheek to get his attention.

"It'll be fine. I know how to take care of me and junior here. I've been to the doctor to find out what I need to do. I just hope your private plane can hold enough water."

"Laney, wow. A baby." He settled down and looked at my stomach. "A baby."

He looked stunned, probably as much as I did when I realized it was true. We'd planned to wait another year or two, but now was just as good. It was what fate had decided for us and we'd learned not to fight against fate too hard. It had brought us together.

Much later, a long flight later, we were in one of the last remaining hotels on the island and looking out at the destruction around us. "It's just so sad, Jake. How are they going to recover from this?"

"I'm working on it. The government has all but abandoned them, but we're here and others are coming. We'll make it right again."

I could see campfires out in the distance belonging to people trying to cook evening meals on the hills they'd run to in order to escape the floods and hadn't left yet. Jake took me in his arms, his hands finding my belly as he did so.

"Don't get too stressed, my love. I know you want to help, but you have more than just you to worry about now." He tucked me against the front of his body delicately, lovingly.

"I just want to go and buy a department store and plunk it down in the square there to give away." I could see the square still littered with debris and the ocean in the distance.

"If that's what you want to do, babe, I'll call my PA in the morning, get him started. Now that we can see exactly what's needed here, we can get started." He pulled me to the bed, and I followed, the exhaustion of a day of travel and then witnessing all of this was taking its toll on me.

I was asleep before I knew it, wrapped in Jake's protective arms. I'd spent a year learning him, loving him, and now I didn't know what I'd do without him. Falling asleep with him was as natural as breathing now. At first, sleeping next to someone had taken some getting used to, but now I couldn't sleep if he wasn't near.

The sun had gone down when I woke up and Jake was behind me, his hands wandering over my back. I felt him hard and thick at my bottom and smiled. Even now, he wanted me. Maybe even as much as I wanted him.

I moved against him to tell him to go deeper, further, and his lips were soon at the back of my neck, doing that thing to me that only he could do. Just a certain spot that he could nip at, bite, or kiss and I was jelly. But only his.

His hand came up to cup a breast, swollen with my new pregnancy, and his soft heat soothed the ache away just as he made a new ache, the ache of desire when his fingers grasped my nipple gently. His touch was different, far gentler than was normal for him, and he was generally quite gentle with me. Except for those times we got lost in a little roughness. I smiled and held my hand over his, letting him know I wanted more, harder.

"I love you, Laney Mallory." He nuzzled the words into my hair before he went back to kissing that spot.

"I love you, Jake Mallory." I pushed my bottom back into him, knowing he loved it.

I wanted to turn into his arms, but this was one of those lazy sessions, those times when you made excruciatingly slow love, and it was perfect. His fingers went down my side, the tingle of skin against skin made me glad I'd gone to sleep naked.

I loved to have my husband touch me and he did it so well. I sighed, content and full of desire as his fingers slid down my thigh, before his fingers were between them, exploring me. I put my right thigh over his, to make room for his wandering fingers. He found the spot he knew I liked the best and started a slow tantalizing circle that soon had me panting.

I concentrated on his fingers, on the sparks he created within me. He left me breathless as his lips found that spot and I let myself go with him.

"Jake, you're so good, baby."

I didn't know what I meant, but he didn't care, he just kept circling, teasing, as I shook in his arms, slow and easy, a soft pinpoint of pleasure. I sighed through it just as softly, letting it pulse through me, a sweetly erotic moment.

"I love hearing you sigh like that. I love feeling you shuddering in my arms." He whispered it at that spot. That one spot that only he had ever found.

"Jake..." I sighed, turning to kiss him, not done at all. I could never get enough of this man.

I might have never known him. I might have ignored Mrs. Mallory's hints about her available grandson. I'd thought she was just trying to get the man out of her basement, I'd had no idea of the gift she was trying to give us both.

He needed to shave but I didn't mind as I found his jawline and cupped it, our tongues meeting as his hands pulled me close. I wouldn't have known what this felt like, to wake up to sex with this incredible man now far more than just my lover. I looked into green eyes when he pulled away and smiled at him.

"Are you worried about the baby?" I asked him as he hesitated, his need clear, but worry clouded his face.

"A little. I know it won't hurt the little thing, but, well, I can't help but worry, can I? You are the love of my life and I have a feeling this little gift we're about to get is going to create even more love. I have to protect you both, you know?" His fingers stroked my cheek and I smiled again.

I was always smiling with him.

"It will be fine, Jake, and I'll tell you if anything hurts, alright? Don't worry now, just love me." I pulled him over me, my thighs falling open to take him into me.

He slid in without guidance, our bodies came together like that now. As if they were each other's home.

I pulled him down to me, I needed to feel surrounded by him, and he came without question. He held me close as our hips moved in time with each other, and my lips found his. I held my hands to his face as he kissed me and our breaths grew ragged together.

Jake was mine, had always been mine. We'd found the perfect rhythm together. I knew, somehow, that we always would.

Jake's pace changed as he drove into me, going deeper, faster until he flipped us, and followed, still merged, to lean back on my hand balanced on his thigh.

"I think we'll have to get used to this position as my belly grows, you know." I gave him a grin and he cupped my breasts as my grin turned dirty. "Apparently pregnancy can make you very horny."

"That's impossible. We'll never be out of bed! All of our friends tease us at it is."

We'd been caught out a few times, at home, in Jake's office, at a gala dinner held at a hotel that we'd had to rent a room in because we just couldn't wait long enough to get home.

"What can I say? You're a sexy guy." I found the perfect angle and the perfect rhythm and started to grind on Jake, the feel of him stretching and stroking all of the best places within me was too much to ignore.

"Or maybe it's that you're one fucking incredible woman, Laney. Fuck, do that again." I'd squeezed him with my muscles and he loved it. I knew he did.

I let my walls flutter around him once more and arched my back, my breasts prominent now. "Touch me, Jake."

I begged my husband for his touch, his soothing stirring touch. Fuck, he drove me insane with it.

We moved together, his hands teasing my nipples, mine propping me up as I fucked him fast and deep until we were both panting as we cried out with shock as pleasure rocked through us. I felt Jake exploding just as I began to pulse around him and we drove each other higher.

I heard him calling my name and squeezed his thigh as he thrust up into me, hard, deep, and I ground my teeth together to keep from screaming out his name. Fuck, he felt so good!

I gave a whine of frustration with being constrained, but I didn't clamp down on my pleasure, I let it roll through me, to the same pace as Jake's driving cock.

Jake made me strive for more, but in a different way to how I'd driven myself my whole life. Instead of driving to be perfect, I sought it out in other forms, in ways I could only achieve with Jake. Ways like this, where we became a whole and I didn't feel so alone. I was perfect already, he'd made me realize, in the way that humans can be perfect, meaning I was more myself now and I was happy with that. He'd made me whole, just as I'd made him whole again.

This is what we were made for. Each other. Nobody could change that. Ever. They could try, but nobody would ever succeed. Not when you had perfect love like this.

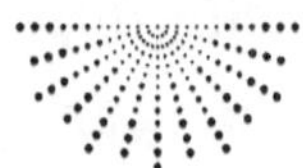

DARK DESIRES
~ A billionaire dark romance series ~
Dark Desire
Dark Rules
Dark Secret
Dark Time
Dark Truth

BARRE TO BAR
~ A billionaire second chance series ~
Dancing With Lies
Dancing With Temptation
Dancing With Doubt
Dancing With Guilt
Dancing With Redemption

TWISTED INTENTION
~ A billionaire revenge romance series ~
Twisted Beauty
Twisted Love
Twisted Fate

Mafia's Obsession
~ A hot mafia romance series ~
Mafia's Dirty Secret
Mafia's Fake Bride
Mafia's Final Play

Screaming Demons
~ An MC romance series full of suspense ~
Rough Start
Rough Ride
Rough Choice
Rough Patch
Rough Return
Rough Road
Rough Trip
Rough Night
Rough Love

Standalone Contemporary Romance
Billionaire in Vegas
Billionaire Hunt

Billionaire's Game
Billionaire Retreat
Billionaire On Air
A Chance To Love
Somebody To Love
Not Mine To Love

Check out Summer's entire collection at
www.summercooper.com/books

ABOUT SUMMER COOPER

Thank you so much for reading. Without you, it wouldn't be possible for me to be a full-time author. I hope you enjoy reading my books as much as I do writing them.

Besides (obviously!) reading and writing, I also love cuddling my dogs, shouting at Alexa, being upside down (aka Yoga) and driving my family cray-cray!

Get in touch at
hello@summercooper.com
www.summercooper.com

facebook.com/summercooperauthor
instagram.com/summercooperauthor
goodreads.com/summercooper
bookbub.com/profile/summer-cooper

9 781917 075442